BECAUSE VENUS CROSSED AN ALPIN VIOLET ON THE DAY THAT I WAS BORN

MONA HØVRING

translated from the Norwegian by
KARI DICKSON & RACHEL RANKIN

BOOK*HUG PRESS
TORONTO 2021
LITERATURE IN TRANSLATION SERIES

First published as Fordi Venus passerte en alpefiol den dagen jeg blei født
by Forlaget Oktober AS, 2018
Published in agreement with Oslo Literary Agency

This translation has been published with the financial
support of NORLA

Library and Archives Canada Cataloguing in Publication

Title: Because Venus crossed an alpine violet on the day I was born /
    Mona Høvring ; translated from the Norwegian by Kari Dickson
    & Rachel Rankin.
Other titles: Fordi Venus passerte en alpefiol den dagen jeg blei født.
    English
Names: Høvring, Mona, author. | Dickson, Kari, translator. | Rankin,
    Rachel, translator.
Series: Literature in translation series.
Description: First English edition. | Series statement: Literature in
    translation series | Translation of: Fordi Venus passerte en
    alpefiol den dagen jeg blei født.
Identifiers: Canadiana (print) 20210252103 | Canadiana (ebook)
    20210252146 | ISBN 9781771667067 (softcover) | ISBN 9781771667074
    (EPUB) | ISBN 9781771667081 (PDF)
Classification: LCC PT8952.18.097 F6713 2021 | DDC 839.823/8—dc23

Printed in Canada

Book*hug Press acknowledges that the land on which we operate is
the traditional territory of many nations, including the Mississaugas
of the Credit, the Anishnabeg, the Chippewa, the Haudenosaunee,
and the Wendat peoples. We recognize the enduring presence of
many diverse First Nations, Inuit, and Métis peoples and are grateful
for the opportunity to meet, work, and learn on this territory.

You get bored with the truck. You push it into a
bramblepatch where it loses balance and falls slowly
over into the tangled branches.

MONIQUE WITTIG, THE OPOPONAX

THE ALPINE VILLAGE

Owing to a mild speech impediment I've had since childhood, I confuse the pronunciation of the author Stefan Zweig's surname with the German word *Schweig*—be quiet. Not that I'm as well-read as I'd like to be, and my German is really rather poor, but I have admired Zweig for a long time. I devour his books and read everything I can find about him. Oh, what a sorrowful end he came to in Rio de Janeiro, and that heart-wrenching suicide note he left: "aus freiem Willen und mit klaren Sinnen." Whenever I throw myself into my own writing, my own attempts to understand the world, there he is, a quiet reminder—*Verwirrung der Gefühle*.

This story begins with me and my sister arriving in an alpine village well into the afternoon. It was winter. The train came to a halt by a station that both slumbered and soared, self-consciously proclaiming its height above sea level.

My sister didn't make the slightest move to help unload our suitcases. She positioned herself on the platform and stood there, completely indifferent, while the conductor helped me with our heavy luggage. I was on the cusp of explaining that she was sick, that she'd just got out of hospital, but contented myself with shaking his hand and saying that I appreciated his thoughtfulness. Before he blew his whistle and boarded the train, the conductor winked at me and wished me good luck. Was it out of pity? Had he understood something I hadn't, seen something I hadn't?

My sister disappeared around the corner of the station building. I had to wheel and carry everything by myself. It was hard going.

In the days before we left, I'd been living in a perpetual daydream. I studied the glossy, seductive brochures we'd been sent. The colour of the sky in the photographs was reminiscent of the light and hue of old films, and the mountains shone with irresistible pinks—they seemed to whisper to me in an unknown language. I pictured an exotic winter wonderland. I dreamt of alpine ski slopes and indoor swimming pools and sophisticated menus curated by expert chefs from the continent. It was like the ecstasy of transformation. I envisioned another epoch.

But it was not an alpine village in some Central European monarchy we'd arrived at, no—my sister couldn't stand air travel, so we were staying in a simple Norwegian village. It lay in splendid isolation at the bottom of a steep mountain, and the people there weren't exactly incomprehensible, but they did speak in a distinctive, slightly drawn-out dialect.

I found my sister by the bus stop. She had positioned herself beside an older woman and a young boy. She looked like any other traveller—nothing suggested instability, nothing screamed hysteria or breakdown. It looked as though she had full control over both time and place, and even though I was outraged by her behaviour, her convincing composure did give me strength. Yes, it pleased me greatly. But I couldn't thank her for the calmness she was emanating, couldn't comment on it. I had to keep my thoughts to myself. Praising her was the same as giving her a task, an obligation. I feared that even the smallest hint of responsibility would whip up her anxiety and contrariness. No, thanking her would ruin everything.

We could see the hotel from the bus stop. It lay a good way up the side of the mountain. It looked like a golden crystal bird, its formidable wings spanning the sheer overhang. I reckoned that it was both rundown and dilapidated now, and its fashionable glory days were long gone. Nevertheless, the building had an alluring splendour about it, illuminated by sunbeams shining with gay abandon. Everything up there in the valley enticed me— harmonious and untouched. It made me think—though not without some resistance—of the doctor who had encouraged us to go, and of Mother who, untroubled, had offered to pay for our stay, as if her freedom could be bought. Freedom from what?

But I didn't get caught up in the question. The magnificent landscape made me feel at peace.

I glanced at my sister. She was standing upright, looking almost distinguished. She made sure to conserve and accentuate her aesthetic qualities: her light grey woollen coat, her large Russian fur hat. She was beautiful, she knew that—beautiful in a certain way.

"This air can cure the sick," I said.

My sister smiled. Her smile resembled the uncontrollable smile that Mother used to wear when she had too little to do.

I thought the hotel up there in the clouds could surely inspire courage in the most wretched of souls. It was an edifying thought.

The bus driver introduced himself over the public address system before insisting that it wasn't dangerous to drive on the steep slopes. You just had to maintain your speed and follow the flow of the curves, he said. He was the loquacious type. He leaned forward and swayed in the soft driver's seat, one hand on the steering wheel and the other holding the microphone. He reminded me of Father. He had the same naive outlook on the world. That's how it seemed. Father is called Roger. Roger Hartmann. Mother's parents thought that Roger was a common, tasteless name. Who was capable of coming up with something like that? Mother is called Karlotta. She was christened Karlotta Kornelia Adelheid.

When Mother was pregnant, she would go to the graveyard. She would wander between the graves for hours, walking up and down until she found names for us, straightforward names, names that suited the people she thought we would be, both inside and out.

My sister's name is Martha. Her hair looks almost white under fluorescent lights. And what is my name? My name is Ella, and my eyes are almost green. I have a book where I write down what I think will happen in the coming year, and on the last day of the year I write down what has actually happened.

Martha had closed her eyes and crossed her arms. I scrutinized her. She was exactly one year older than me, though I was taller—not by much, but enough for Martha to be constantly irked by it. Our birthday was the same date, the eighth of October. We had been close as children, living as though we were twins. We were together day and night, and even slept in the same bed until we were well into our teens. So what happened between Martha and me? I'd thought that we would be together forever, that we would study together and have boyfriends we both liked. But one grey afternoon, Martha came home and said she wanted to quit her job. She worked in a perfumery and had long hinted that she was fed up, so that in itself wasn't a surprise, but then she told us she was getting married, that this was the reason—and that was something nobody in the family had seen coming.

"I'm moving to Denmark," she said.

As she stood in the bedroom, packing toiletries and clothes into a bag, she behaved as though entranced. I clung to her, threw my arms around her neck, bawling, but she loosened my grip. She seemed cold and unfeeling. Then she shrugged, as she was wont to do, and left.

I also quit my job the next day. Since finishing high school, I'd worked in the hardware store that stood wall-to-wall with the perfumery. Neither Mother nor Father tried to convince me to stay on. Mother said I could stay at home for as long as I wanted. So I stayed at home. Everything was ruined for me when Martha left. I couldn't even walk past her room without feeling dizzy. We lived in a large, old wooden house. Yes, it was an enormous house. Father used to say that Martha and I ruled the east wing while he and mother were ensconced in the west wing. At a later point, Mother moved down to the ground floor—she wanted to sleep in peace, as she put it—but Martha was the first to actually leave home.

One day, I walked past the perfumery and was so overcome with wooziness that I had to lie down on the pavement so as not to fall. I must have looked crazy or drunk, lying there. The spell was distressing. I couldn't stand losing control, so I stopped wandering the streets I'd previously loved to visit. I mostly stayed at home, listening to the radio, reading, occasionally watching a film. I was desperate for any alleviation, and even sought a cure in homeopathic medicine. To be fair, I didn't know what it could have helped with. I told the homeopath

I was dizzy. The homeopath looked into my eyes and asked me a load of questions.

"I'm dizzy," I repeated. "I'm light-headed."

No, I didn't go insane, but I missed Martha. It was a terrible time. I realized I had to rein in my loss. And fortunately, I managed to do so. I showed my loss respect. I took it seriously. I allowed myself to rest and take it easy for the entire autumn, as though I were sick.

I have never understood what actually happened to my sister. She just left. It was as though her heart had been replaced, as though everything inside her grew cold. And her self-destructive fantasy, this fervent infatuation, was directed toward a strange, unattractive man who was also her boss's ex. How could a young woman allow herself to be seduced by a man like that, a boring and pompous Casaubon? It was as though Martha herself didn't understand it. And when she came back, because of course she came back, she was withdrawn and didn't tell anybody anything. She was sullen and sardonic, almost aggressive. Perhaps it was her way of expressing her shame. I was dismayed by her behaviour but also hungry for answers. What had she experienced without me? Where had her friendliness gone? Where had her love gone? Her devotion? But I bit my tongue. There was a rigidity about her that stopped me. And this distance between us persisted.

I was the one who accompanied Martha to the sanatorium. The doctor gave a kind of speech while she admitted her. She tilted her head and spoke with great zeal. She said that Martha had had a breakdown, the kind of breakdown that can affect absolutely anyone. Even the strongest of people can find themselves in situations where they need help. I thought what the doctor said was self-evident, but she was an authority unto herself. She was both careful and decisive.

"We have to learn how best to steal back our hearts," she said.

"To hell with the heart," Martha said.

"I see," the doctor said. "By the way, your father says hello. He's phoned several times. Your mother has, too."

"Father and Mother can get stuffed," Martha said.

"I see," said the doctor. "You're one of them."

"What do you mean?" Martha snapped.

But the doctor was not at all bothered by her obnoxious behaviour. "You are ill," she said. "It'll be a long time before you realize that it's a gift."

She took Martha's pulse and asked her to open her mouth and stick out her tongue while she continued the lecture.

"You need rest," the doctor said. "You need to be idle. Idleness is underrated. Plus, people would rather not know about the troubles of others. It's often only the parents who are able to see the beauty in their lost children."

"I can't breathe," Martha said.

"And yet you are breathing," the doctor said. "Now you need time to find something that makes you feel grateful."

Martha laughed feebly.

"At least I know which medicines not to give you," the doctor said. "Either all will be well or it will pass."

Well, that was a strange mantra, I thought.

After having accompanied Martha to the ward, the doctor phoned for a taxi for me. I thanked her, inadvertently adding that she had a lovely profile.

"It really is aerodynamic," I said.

I have a real talent for spouting nonsense when I get nervous. I take after Father.

Her smile surprised me. It was charming—almost too much of a good thing.

I slammed the car door behind me. The driver glanced at me in the mirror, irritated. But I didn't apologize. No, I didn't apologize.

One day in early February, I got a call from the doctor. She said Martha would soon be discharged and asked if I could possibly accompany her to the mountains, to an excellent hotel where we could spend a few weeks. The doctor knew the woman who ran the place—an old friend, apparently—and she had spoken with Mother, who had said I could no doubt go with Martha. She needed to have someone with her, now that she was so disturbed. It was Mother who had used that expression, not the doctor, as I understood it. And Mother would gladly pay for our stay.

"So I'm going to be an escort?" I said. "A career I've always dreamed of."

I don't know if it was first and foremost for Martha's sake or if it was to make an impression on this doctor, but whatever the reason, I promptly agreed to travel to the mountains with my sister.

But the next day, I felt a weight pressing down on me. Our old wooden villa, that huge, dilapidated building, smelled bilious and musty. I now deeply regretted my benevolence. The doctor had been so seductive. She had a kind of audacious and measured charm. I was even taken by her voice on the telephone. I really couldn't cancel the trip she had suggested. To change my mind and not go now would be embarrassing. Naturally, I didn't want to show myself in a bad light. I lay down on the sofa in the living room. Everything was magnified. Everything I thought, everything I imagined, was exaggerated, extreme. Everything inside me and around me was stupefied with dejection and dust.

When we passed the treeline, the gnarled trees with their frozen, sap-covered twigs finally loosened their grip. The bus driver put the microphone in the holder on the dashboard. He sat with both hands on the steering wheel, concentrating fully on the final stretch. I yawned deeply. The sky had darkened. No stars shone. I was filled with both anticipation and exhaustion. I took a bag of sweet liquorice from my handbag.

Soon we would be there. Soon we would be able to sleep. The winter would not last forever. We would rest and dream about spring. The light would throw itself across the footpaths. The brooks would rejoice. The waterfalls would cascade happily.

I have an aptitude for logic. I've always liked calculating things. Algebra calms me. I had long dreamed of applying for a Master of Science in mathematics up north. It wasn't just an impulse—I've always been gifted when it comes to numbers—but at the time, I wasn't sure what I wanted to be. I'm still not sure. There was a period when I considered becoming a garbage collector. The working hours and freedom associated with the job appealed to me and, in addition, a job like that would have strengthened my muscles and calmed my soul. It was a comforting thought. Or perhaps I could be a gardener? That had always seemed like a promising job to me. Apart from when I thought about worms and ants and wasps and flies and mouse droppings and bird shit. Or what about becoming a nun? What about living a chaste and modest life? No. First, I wanted to be intense and amorous. First, I wanted to live indecently. *Indecently.* Such a great word. I could also imagine being an electrician. Or an ornithologist? Just the word *ornithologist* was enough to conjure romantic notions in me. But I knew nothing about birds. I was actually scared of them, especially seagulls. I was afraid of seagulls and knives. To be fair, I still am. Once, when I was nine years old, I cut myself horribly. The vegetable knife was newly sharpened and keen. I wasn't concentrating. My grip slipped. The sound of the blade meeting my finger was like a soft, nauseating squelch. Mother wasn't home, but fortunately Martha managed to keep calm and acted quickly. She wrapped a bandage around my injured finger and taped it up. In next to no time, she had bound it in plastic wrap and soft cloths, which she then put into a bag filled with ice cubes. She phoned for a taxi, and when we got to Emergency, she was praised for being so clear-headed. I personally wasn't so robust. I *ouched* and *owed* as my fingertip was sewn back on.

As a result, I have struggled to look at open wounds without being disgusted. I realized I could never be a doctor, even though the career enticed me for various reasons. I liked the thought of being able to heal, and I have always liked wearing white clothes.

THE
GLASS
HOTEL

The hotel was even more grandiose than I'd imagined. It reminded me of those enormous oriental birdcages that often take up the whole room. A huge glass veranda had been built along the side that faced the valley. Panes of glass, framed by white wooden battens, shone fiercely in the darkness. I found the location attractive. Who had dreamt up this palace?

It was like Martha was sleepwalking. The only thing she took from the bus was her coat. The driver helped me carry the luggage into the brightly lit foyer. He stood there, as though stunned, and looked around. It was like he didn't want to leave. But when a slender woman with an elegant updo came into the reception, he bowed quickly and bounded away like a frightened hare. The woman greeted and welcomed us warmly. She had appeared like a ghost, just like Mother used to appear back home. She wasn't there, and then suddenly, out of nowhere, there she was. I thought the woman was about the same age as Mother, perhaps a few years younger. She moved with a gracefulness that was in keeping with the splendid, yet slightly faded, surroundings.

Once a year, every autumn, Mother booked a table at one of the restaurants in town, a place she had frequented in her younger days. For some unknown reason, considering the reputation of the place was no more than average, there was always caviar on the menu, and Mother took advantage of the opportunity. I still remember, and not without some pleasure, the first time we went to the restaurant.

As soon as the waiter came, the fun started. Mother wagged her index finger at the open menu.

"What's the caviar like?" she asked.

"What's the caviar like?" the waiter repeated.

"I'm rather fussy when it comes to caviar," Mother said.

"It's caviar," the waiter said warily.

"Yes, but is it from France? From Gironde? Is it from Russia? From Kazakhstan?"

And she didn't let it go. Was the caviar fresh? Were the eggs large or small? Was it Ossetra, Sevruga, or Beluga?

At this point in the conversation, the waiter was showing clear signs of unease. His forehead began to gleam, as though the heat were rising from the table before the food had even been served.

"What about asparagus instead?" he suggested.

"No," said Mother. "Now that I have this extraordinary craving for caviar, nothing can stop me. No matter. I'll take the caviar."

"Would you like vodka with it?" the waiter asked.

"No, I don't drink alcohol," Mother said. "But I would like the sausage with vinaigrette dressing for my main course. And the girls must have pork cutlets."

Martha and I followed carefully. We really enjoyed this moment.

"Well, that's that," Mother said, after the empty dessert bowls had been taken away. She sighed with something that resembled happiness when she asked for the bill. And the waiter cheered up as she handed him the banknotes. She tipped generously. Mother was a queen. She was like an art nouveau building: no hard lines, no corners. She consisted only of soft, rolling shapes. She was like a swaying plant, waving magnificently in the wind. And she had slightly protuberant eyes. They made her look extremely beautiful.

Oh, why did I always associate the world with Mother? I wanted to stop thinking about her, I really did, so it had to be possible.

"I've given you the best," said the woman in reception without explaining what "the best" was, or what this goodwill implied.

She pointed and led the way up a wide staircase. The ornate bannister cast shadows across the steps. People who died long ago looked down at us from the paintings arranged along the hall. It was as though they were showing us the way as well. Perhaps death was the most blissful thing that had happened to them. But where did I get all these lamentable thoughts from?

We walked some way down a carpeted corridor. The walls were cream, with a border of golden flowers just below the cornice on the high ceiling. The pale chandeliers clinked softly above us as the woman stopped in front of one of the dark wooden doors. The brass plate said number 12. The woman opened the door and turned on the light. She leaned forward, as though she were about to either hit me or caress me, and pressed the key into my hand with a gentle, almost indecent touch. She still hadn't introduced herself. I decided to call her Ruth. I usually gave names to people I didn't know. Once again, she welcomed us, nodded sharply, and disappeared.

It turned out we'd been given a suite with a bedroom, a charming living room, and an enormous tiled bathroom. These breathtaking rooms with a view were divided by sliding doors, which Martha immediately slid open. The arched windows stretched almost from floor to ceiling. The wallpaper looked like embroidered illustrations of

Baroque gardens. The sconces had several arms and emitted a soft light. Someone had fired up the ceramic stove in the biggest room, and in the bathroom, just in front of one of the windows that faced the village and the valley, sat a majestic bathtub that made even Martha gasp, enthralled. She immediately put the plug in and turned on the taps. A glass jar of turquoise bath salts had been placed on a stool. Two dressing gowns made of thick, white terry cloth hung on the door. Martha threw off her clothes and stood naked while she poured the bath salts into the water. The water foamed and filled the room with steam and aroma.

While Martha bathed, I unpacked. I smelled a slight hint of musk in the wardrobe. I hung our coats and dresses on the sturdy hangers and placed our tops and underwear in the chest of drawers.

Martha took her time. After unpacking, I managed to eat two apples from the overflowing fruit bowl and read a long chapter from the book I'd brought with me. When Martha finally emerged from the bathroom, her face was shining, her otherwise pale cheeks rosy.

Martha and I hadn't slept in the same room for a long time, but now we crept into the huge bed without discussion. The mattress was hard, just how I liked it. The linen bedsheets were both snug and cool, newly ironed yet still slightly creased.

When we were little girls, Martha and I were convinced that the sofa in the living room was cursed. Everyone who sat on it got tired—you simply had to lie down and give in to sleep. Mother surrendered herself completely to this mysterious piece of furniture. When she came home late from work, she would settle down on the sofa with duvets and pillows and sheets.

Once, having read about feng shui in an interior design magazine, Martha and I moved the sofa. Inspired by the advice about the placement of furniture and the influential power of physical surroundings, we decided to turn the sofa so it faced the window on the south wall. But then everything changed. Mother barely slept. She became sluggish and irritable. She stopped talking about herself, stopped asking how we were, and was no longer interested in what we were thinking. Martha and I moved the sofa back one night when we were unable to sleep, as Mother had spoken about the future with such bitter pessimism.

There was a knock at the door. Before we managed to answer, Ruth came in. She placed a tray between us and poured hot chocolate from a porcelain teapot into two gold-rimmed cups. And as we lay there, with this stranger bending over us, I felt there was almost something daring about her small, reliable movements. I wasn't cold, but I was trembling. A bowl of whipped cream sat on the tray. I couldn't resist. I stuck my finger in and tasted it.

"Melancholic people in particular need something sweet," Ruth said, before leaving us as quickly as she had come.

Martha and I slowly drank ourselves calm, then placed the empty cups on our bedside tables. We didn't brush our teeth, didn't close the curtains—we just wrapped the duvets even tighter around our bodies and lay there, looking at ourselves in the tall mirror that was placed on the long wall just beside the bed.

"We're two cherubs now," Martha said.

It was the most cheerful thing she'd said in a long time.

I woke up in the middle of the night. A latch had come undone and one of the small upper windows was banging. The mist had drifted into the room, wrapping itself around the furniture. I glanced over at Martha. I wanted to stroke her forehead, but I resisted. Instead, I got up. I opened the heavy wardrobe doors. The scent of musk was still there. It filled me with yearning, only I didn't know what I was yearning for. I felt like I'd landed in an unfamiliar era. My head felt empty. My body was disconnected. It was as though death were trying to take me. Death, with its joyful malice. This was how I daydreamed. This was how I tried to hold on to the world.

It was all I could do. I realized I had to learn to suppress these emotions. I felt frail and tired. Imagine being able to rest, at least while you are asleep.

Martha was snoring gently, muffled, as though she was humming. She still had her makeup on. She'd always used a concealer that was a touch too light. Her lipstick was smeared. She didn't look like an angel anymore. She looked like one of Dracula's doomed brides. An aura of hunger surrounded her.

The morning light flooded into the dining room. I hated the morning light—it made me think of X-rays. I regretted not bringing sunglasses with me. I'd have to see if I could buy a pair—there must surely be an optician down in the village. I felt like I was on a stage. The glass wall that faced onto the shining valley, cloaked in white, made me feel ill. Fortunately, it was winter—the nice weather couldn't possibly last.

I hurried toward an empty table, nodding at the other guests—a few old couples and a family with two small children. I put my bag down, got myself some coffee, juice, and cutlery, and piled a large plate with scrambled eggs and bacon. Where was Martha? I ate with a voracious appetite, pushed the plate away, and fetched another cup of coffee as well as two moist chocolate croissants. I ate both of them quickly. It's strange—that's how it's been my whole life. No matter what mood I'm in, I've always had an incredible appetite, and if it weren't for my extremely high metabolism, I'd probably have been a fat and lethargic girl.

I picked flakes of puff pastry from the plate, swung back on my chair, and immediately noticed a person on the other side of the room. A young man. He was slim and elegant. He wore a brown tweed suit and a yellow sweater with a high neck. His hair was cut short, but he had a long fringe that fell across his face. I wanted to sit closer, to study him. Did he have high cheekbones? What did his wrists look like? I squinted carefully, but the light was in my eyes and I couldn't get a proper look at him.

Martha arrived. She was suddenly standing in front of me, asking if I'd eaten. I pointed at the leftovers of my meal. Martha said it would have been nice to eat together. She apparently deemed it appropriate to feel put out. I didn't reply. We hadn't had meals together since she went her own way.

"You look good," I said.

"It's because I've started drinking again," said Martha.

"I didn't know you'd stopped," I said.

"You're never going to know everything about me," she said, wanting to sting me with her secrets.

I turned away, pulled a hair tie from my bag, and gathered my hair into a bun. I concentrated on being distant—distant gaze, distant body language. I wanted to get even with her. I wanted to make her feel insignificant, disregarded—I knew how little it took.

I stroked the white tablecloth.

"I didn't mean to hurt you," Martha said.

She seemed sincere. But I wasn't ready to give in to her just like that.

"That's when you do the most damage," I said.

Martha shivered and buttoned her new cashmere coat. "There's such a draught here," she said.

"Breakfast is actually finished," I said. "If you're hungry, you'll have to hurry up."

"I'm not feeling well," said Martha.

She asked if I could perhaps get her some food and read the day's newspapers to her. I got up from the table and did as she said. I couldn't be bothered arguing. I placed the overflowing plate in front of her and she asked me to pass her the salt. She ate while I rattled off the news. I only read the headlines and the first paragraphs. That was enough for Martha.

The young man left the dining room. The breakfast was cleared away by two women in light blue dresses and white aprons. I decided to go for a walk. I wanted to take a stroll down to the village without telling Martha. I wanted to do some shopping, try on sunglasses, take in the surroundings.

It took a good hour to walk from the hotel down to the centre. The road was freshly cleared, the valley quiet and friendly. The snow-covered trees were like free spirits; it was as though they had let go of all their sorrows, all their regret. They let the winter sun flow through them, through everything they were, generously making space for the light. The trees wanted for nothing—all they had to let go of was their delicate pine cones and soft needles. I stopped beside a running brook, bent down, and drank from both hands. It was good, and it was painful. My mouth was numbed. It looked like the water was electric. The movements in the wetness were careful, the small gusts of wind over the cold vapour of the surface merely hinting at their existence. A pile of newly felled logs smelled so strong that it seemed unnatural. I've never really felt much of a pull toward nature. Quite the opposite, in fact—I liked cities, the bigger the better. There was something calming about the crowds of people in the city streets—calming and indifferent. It suited me. But now I was so engrossed in everything I saw and the feeling of being alone in this wild landscape that I jumped when a sudden noise disturbed the peace. A motorbike sailed by at great speed. I watched it pass. The driver wasn't wearing a helmet. A bit farther down the road, he swerved to a halt. I recognized the young man from breakfast. He gestured over his shoulder with his thumb. I understood that there was space for a passenger. But I waved him onward. Even though I was curious about him, I wasn't going to gamble with my life just to get to know him. He revved the engine with determination and continued at breakneck speed down the winding road.

There wasn't a single house between the hotel and the church. Or maybe they were just snowed under. What did I know? Perhaps there were people living in the space below, waiting for spring: a mother, sitting at the kitchen table with a stack of unpaid bills, boisterous children rushing around with superhero figures, an old man standing at the window, staring at the snow pressing against the pane. I liked to let such fantasies flow freely. I let them take up residence in me. When I did that, I kept myself sane.

I turned around and tried to catch sight of the hotel, but it was hidden behind an overhang. Before, I couldn't understand people who went wandering about in the mountains. Now I could imagine staying up here for months. I felt like I was in such good form—I was barely out of breath. I bent down and stroked a little bright green spruce shoot that was sticking out of the snow. How many metres above sea level was I, actually?

The church towered up from the mountainside, surrounded by a graveyard that looked as though it could, at any moment, go sliding down into the village with everything it contained. I pushed open the wrought-iron gates that led to the dead and took a detour through the graves. Small lanterns had been lit in certain places, and wreaths and flower arrangements made of pine branches and purple heather had been placed here and there by the headstones. I stopped beside a modest memorial. "District Doctor," it said, then the name, then the dates 1881–1978, and beneath that, in worn, gold lettering: "Sometimes heal. Often soothe. Always comfort."

From where I was standing, I had a great view of the village. People were moving around down there like small, slow animals. I hoped I wouldn't die during the summer. If it were up to me, I would want to die in January or February. Nothing happened during those two months anyway.

When I was a child, I read the story of Heidi until the book was falling apart. I was forever dreaming about living with a grandfather in a cabin up in the Swiss Alps. These reveries made me feel slightly guilty because Mother and Father were nice enough. But my longing was stronger than my bad conscience, and I became infatuated with my dreams. I made idyllic drawings of the grandfather's goats and of Peter, the goatherd who looked after them. I drew the blind grandmother with her arms full of bread rolls. I drew the young girl, Clara, who was in a wheelchair. And, with morbid fascination, I sketched Heidi's evil aunt. I lost myself in dreams of wintry, star-filled skies and sleigh rides and powder snow. I longed to lean into the grandfather's embrace, wrapped up in sheepskin and wool.

I left the graveyard with a feeling of freedom, as though I'd found a solution. It was a paradoxical sensation, a kind of agitation, like a lightweight object, as though I were carrying an enormous, almost weightless block of porous stone. It was as though everything inside me were crackling. I didn't struggle. I moved as though hypnotized. My nervous system was splintering. I was forced to stop. I had to compose myself. I glanced in all directions. And the mere act of standing there, breathing, gave me a kind of loathsome happiness. But I soon realized that this happiness could not last. The burden would have been too great—my cells would have been shot to pieces.

I soon passed the patisserie on the square. In the middle of a little park was an ice-covered pond where the winter birds flitted about. An older man stopped in front of me and held out a bread roll. He asked in English if I wanted it. I felt uncomfortable. I liked neither pushy men nor flocks of birds. When I didn't reply, the man took a step closer, still with the piece of bread in his hand, and asked again if I wanted it. Goodness gracious, did I look so pitiful?

"No thanks, I'm not hungry," I said, and hurried onward. Only when the park was behind me did I realize that the man had offered me food to give to the birds.

I went into the patisserie. Even though I'd eaten a lot for breakfast, I was hungry again, hungry for something sweet, and, in any case, I was freezing. I bought two sizable Danish pastries and found an empty table. I kept both my hat and coat on because every time the door opened, a cold gust rushed into the premises.

Mother believed that a house should be kept cool. She used to say that thoughts became woolly in the warmth. And anything could happen in the heat. Eighteen degrees Celsius was the maximum indoor temperature Mother allowed, but both Martha and I preferred twenty-three. This disagreement drove Martha and me to visit the local pool several times a week. On the weekends, we were usually the first to arrive and the last to leave.

And before school, we'd hang around in secret beside the bakery, where the warm air from the ovens wafted out of the air vents. Once, I saw a black-brown rat dash along the wall. It shocked me that it could be found there, so close to all the white, so close to the flour and the iced buns and the baker's clean clothes.

While I ate the pastries, I ruminated on what to do during my little trip into the centre. I was going to get new sunglasses—that was already planned—but I also wanted to stop by a hairdresser. I decided I wanted short hair. I don't know why. After all, that's something you do in the summer, in the warmth, so you can feel the sun properly. Perhaps I was inspired by the young man at breakfast. Sometimes I'm so easily influenced. No, it had nothing to do with him, and anyway, I didn't want a long fringe. I thought my spontaneity would annoy Martha. That's why I wanted to cut my hair off, not right down the skull, it wasn't that dramatic, but it was irrational—I wanted my hair cut short in order to keep a distance from my sister. I wanted to draw a line. I didn't want to allow her stubborn dejection to devour me. Or was it my own stubborn dejection I wanted to mark and protect? As a child, I was able to control my sorrows. As a child, I belonged to Martha and Mother and Father. In precisely that order. As a child, I felt pretty and lucky and wise. Now, I felt pathetic. Over the last few months, I'd hardly been able to be with people. I just wanted to rest and drink wine and not think, really. But now, I wanted to cut my hair. Now, I wanted to buy new sunglasses, and maybe find a pair of bottle-green leather gloves as well.

I went to the washroom and washed the sticky sugar and pastry grease from my fingers. Then I went to the optician. The selection wasn't overwhelming, but I found what I was looking for in the very first display case—a pair of large, round black glasses that Mother would have called film-star glasses. The buxom woman behind the till praised my choice.

"Those glasses were made for you," she said.

I thanked her for the compliment and pulled out my card without asking how much they cost.

Right beside the optician was a barber, and I thought it made the most sense to go there, given that I'd decided on a boyish cut.

I was led to an empty chair by a good-natured fellow of almost sixty. He had white hair that stuck straight up. And as soon as he got going with the scissors, he started waxing on about how he was able to read people's thoughts through their hair.

"You see," he said, "the hair goes right down into the head, and then it transmits messages from the brain up to me. You can believe what you want, but I know what goes on inside people's heads."

I sat there and hoped he wouldn't start telling me about my inner workings. I wouldn't be able to answer back. But there were no interpretations, no analysis of my soul.

Right in the middle of cutting my hair, the hairdresser disappeared into a backroom. He turned on some music and came back, clearly satisfied, almost enthusiastic.

> Gracias a la vida que me ha dado tanto
> Me dio dos luceros, que cuando los abro
> Perfecto distingo lo negro del blanco
> Y en el alto cielo su fondo estrellado
> Y en las multitudes el hombre que yo amo

He asked if I knew who Violeta Parra was. I couldn't answer. I didn't understand what was wrong with me. I bowed my head and clutched my chest with both hands. I started to cry. The biggest tear that flowed out of me was like a colourless marble, a silvery-grey pearl. I felt a pang of grief. I cried and cried. I wanted to get out of there. Mother of God. I had a revelation: one can fall apart at absolutely anything.

As it turned out, Ruth was called Ruth. I've always loved coincidences like that. I'd just got back from my shopping trip when I ran into her outside the little chapel situated just beside the hotel. I couldn't resist. I asked her straight out what her name was, and she replied that her name was Ruth, and apparently didn't notice how much it thrilled me. Then she told me about this peculiar little place of worship of unknown origin. Nobody knew who had built it. It was an enigma, a mystery.

"Does anyone use it?" I asked.

"Use it?"

"For communion and things like that?" I said.

Ruth said the chapel was open day in, day out, all year round. Then she walked toward the hotel as if someone had called for her while I remained standing in front of the unlocked door. I couldn't bring myself to enter. I had no reason to, other than curiosity, which I kept in check. In any case, I didn't like the thought of being in there by myself. I wasn't superstitious, but all the same.

When I got back to the room, Martha's mood had improved. She was more talkative than she'd been in a long time. She was sitting there, watching a documentary about remote farms.

"Oh my God," she said. "Why do people paint their houses dark red? It looks like blood."

Her joviality made me more daring, and I took the opportunity to unsettle her a little. I removed my outside clothes, pulled off my hat, and put it on the shelf in the wardrobe. I fixed my short hair. Martha looked at me drowsily.

"It suits you," she said, changing the channel.

"Thanks," I said, and opened a bottle of wine. I poured two glasses and offered her one.

Martha drank wine like she drank water, quickly and greedily. She was sitting in the deep, plush armchair, engrossed in the program.

The only letter she sent me after she left home was postmarked Copenhagen. She wrote that she was pregnant, she was going to have twins. She was incredibly happy, she wrote, and the children, they were going to be so beautiful. I thought she was lying, that she was neither happy nor pregnant. And when she came home just a few weeks later, she seemed almost insane. She was worn down and hotheaded. It was heartbreaking to see her like that. She swamped me with her woes. Her anxiety became mine. She couldn't handle being contradicted. If I made even the slightest objection, she vilified me. She threw things at me. She was impossible to placate. And I couldn't protect myself. I just took it, as though it were my duty, as though I owed her something. Martha had power over me. I loved her. I don't know where these stupid, sanctimonious thoughts came from, but I decided I would never betray her the way she had betrayed me. I would put up with her impulses. I wouldn't give up on her. And what did I know? Who can ever truly empathize with the pain of another person?

Even though I've always liked things to be tidy—my room, the bathroom, the kitchen cupboards—I've never managed to dispose of the debris and detritus within my soul, which I've carried with me since I was a young girl. And the annoying thing is that it mostly concerns trivialities—Martha's acerbic comments, Mother's mystifying impulses, Father's carefree ways.

I remember there was a time when Martha had invited her class over for a party. It must have been in autumn, possibly late August. The south side of the house was a proliferation of poppies, marigolds, and cornflowers. Martha and I had cut the flowers and put them into a large glass bowl full of water. I remember we discussed which sounded better: "collecting" or "cutting." No, "gathering" sounded nicest. "Gathering" was what we decided on. It was the most graceful expression.

While we were busy decorating the living room, Mother arrived home. She looked so exhausted. She was shivering, lightly dressed, as always.

"What are you doing?" she asked.

"I've gathered flowers," said Martha.

"I'm so bloody fed up with all these celebrations of yours," said Mother.

Without warning, Martha shoved the glass bowl onto the floor so that water and flowers and sharp, shining shards flowed over my feet. She ran out of the room. I looked down at my soaking wet tights. What was it that had pierced my heart? Not Mother's careless remark, and not the smashed bowl, no—it was Martha who had disappointed me. It was Martha who had taken the credit for the work we had done together, work we had both enjoyed.

"We gathered the flowers," I said. "Both of us did."

Mother shrugged. She turned around and went into the kitchen without saying a word.

Was she really so unmoved?

I stamped recklessly across the floor, opened the sliding door that led to the garden, and sat down on the grass. A piece of glass had got lodged in the sole of my foot. The pain was hellish, and it took some time before I managed to pull out the shard.

I thought I would never forget my sorrows. It was a frightful discovery: to have cheeks that bloomed like flowers.

When I went to bed, I was spent and fell asleep after just a few minutes. But I woke up in the middle of the night, feeling rested. I got up and dressed myself. I was quiet and efficient. I wanted to go to the chapel. It was just an impulse, really. But Martha woke up when I opened the door to the hallway. She propped herself up on her elbows and asked what I was doing. I said I couldn't sleep. She said, "Wait," and swung her legs out of the bed. She wanted to come with me.

It was bitterly cold outside. The air was so refreshing that I couldn't help saying it was like champagne. Martha sighed but put up with my exuberance. She didn't criticize it.

We climbed like cats up the snow-covered steps that led to the little place of worship. Someone had made snow lanterns that glowed on either side of the door. We went inside and we each lit a candle. Russian icons hung on the walls, and an enormous, seven-armed brass candelabra sat on the altar. Or was it made of gold?

Everything was glittering, as though we found ourselves in the middle of a swarm of twinkling insects or inside a crowd of silent stars.

"To the future," I said, tilting my candle toward Martha's. "To the birds and to peace," I added.

"You're such a fool," said Martha.

"Do you think we could bear to see the face of God?" I said.

Martha sat down on one of the narrow, unsteady wooden pews.

I babbled away: Did Martha know that protons and electrons are some of the most constant things in existence? Did she remember that Asian film we'd seen when we were children, the one with the two blind masseurs? They were out walking along a mountain trail when one of them said to the other: "What a view! It's like we can see!"

"The man I moved away with," Martha interrupted.

I leaned forward and studied one of the small icons.

"He believed that women were basically a burden," she continued. "He claimed I didn't have any ambitions, but I did have ambitions. I dreamt about all manner of things: about having children and someone to love me, about jewellery and travelling and fame."

"Fame?" I said.

"You know I have a great singing voice."

"Oh, right?" I said.

I felt like Martha was reeling off a bizarre confession. It was both heartfelt and simple. It seemed easy to forgive her there and then. I was tempted to wrap my arms around her, but I contented myself with sitting beside her. I stared at the two candles we'd lit. It was like we were children again. A joyfulness came over me, and when we stood outside in the light of the moon, I asked her if she could also hear the murmurs of the dead.

Martha didn't reply.

"I think nature is sinister," I said. "And God makes us tired."

We came to the bottom of the steep steps. Our shadows in the snow made me think of strange seraphim, uninvited guests. A cat darted across the mounds of snow that had been cleared from the road, quick as lightning. We halted abruptly. Then another cat shot out. Cats are so fearless, in the same way I thought Father was fearless when I was a young girl. Father was so smart and resourceful. He could defend me against all the threats of the world, I thought at the time. Father often said I was gifted. He claimed I was wiser than he was, more dynamic. He could say things like I was young, and that he would soon die—he was forever saying that he would soon die. And every time I forgot myself and asked him for advice about one thing or another, he would say that

I should never ask him for advice about anything. He called me "treasure," "little supernova," "little heart," "little lamb." "Oh, you crumpled caramel wrapper," he called me, "little hazelnut," "little sugar cookie," and "old crow." "I've always said that pain is experience and it pours in to fill an empty space." He could come out with things like that. I thought that Father was like a cat—tenacious and lithe and domineering.

When we let ourselves into the room, Martha asked if I could go down and get her a bottle of water. She didn't like drinking from the tap. You never knew what sediment might remain in the old pipes, she said, and anyway, she wanted sparkling water. Ruth had told us we could help ourselves from the fridge in reception. We just had to write a note and leave it in the bowl on the counter. There was no nightshift. It was a simple and trusting system.

For the second time that night, I opened the door to the hallway, the chandeliers clinking softly again. I crept down the stairs with the ornate bannister. There was a room, an office, behind the reception desk. The door was ajar and the light was on. It struck me that Martha and I might have woken Ruth up with our nocturnal excursion. I knocked on the door tentatively and pushed it open, wanting to explain myself and apologize for the disturbance. Over by a large desk stood two figures, locked in a tight embrace. One of them was Ruth. The other had their back to me, but I recognized the tweed suit and the yellow polo neck. It was the young man from breakfast. Ruth looked at me. Her gaze was matter-of-fact, as though she were awaiting practical instructions. The young man turned around, also unperturbed. His jacket was open and his polo neck was pulled up. Now I saw it, clear as day—it wasn't a young man, but a woman, slim and boyish, true enough, with small breasts, but a woman nonetheless. She pulled down her jumper, tightened her belt around her waistband, and pushed her fringe back. Ruth cleared her throat and asked, still pinning me with her practical gaze, if I needed anything.

"I was just getting a bottle of water," I said.

"Help yourself," said Ruth.

I was about to retreat when the young woman took a few steps toward me and held out her hand.

I took hold of it. It was a reflex.

"Dani," she said, bowing.

"Dani?" I said.

"Dani," she repeated. "My name's actually Daniella, but you know how it is."

I said goodnight, backed out of the room, and closed the door, a bit too hard.

Martha was asleep when I got back to the room. I put the bottle of water on her bedside table. Once again, she'd gone to bed without removing her makeup, her pillowcase smeared with lipstick. What was she thinking? I felt a burdensome tenderness for her, a tenderness that was neither gentle nor good-hearted, but a tenderness nonetheless. On the day she left, I had to curb my self-righteousness. Self-righteousness is a colour that nobody suits. I wished I were stronger. I forgot that some people lived as though they were in a dream. But I kept up the facade. I embraced the feeling of being abandoned with hard-won dignity, my inner tremors hidden as best I could. And I succeeded. I fooled Mother, I fooled Father, I even fooled myself. That was how I survived that time. That was how I survived my loss and the strained, furious tenderness I felt for my sister.

A DOOR IS EITHER OPEN OR CLOSED

Despite my midnight wanders, I woke up early the next morning. I turned on the shower, stayed under the warm water for a long time, then afterwards stretched and loosened my limbs. I stood in the middle of the bathroom and kept my legs straight as I bent over and touched my toes with my fingertips. When Mother worked as a nurse, she often talked about how important it was to get the blood flowing. She was an enterprising lady, particularly when she worked as a carer. She looked after a young woman for an extended period of time. The woman had a muscle-wasting disease that would eventually kill her, but it was a slow process because her heart was strong and steady. She looked like a bag of bones, a ghost. She lay in her bed with a faint and friendly smile, just withering away. Both Martha and I, who had a habit of popping in to see Mother at work, noticed her husband gazing longingly at her, and he was open about it and used every opportunity to stroke her arm or back, under the guise of gratitude. He nestled up to her, and she let him, just laughed drily at his advances; in fact, she looked rather satisfied on the occasions when he gave her flowers and expensive chocolates. Mother cut and arranged the flowers in vases, which she then placed all around the house that wasn't ours. She flirted and fooled around. Martha and I thought the man was contrived and overly familiar, that he had discovered Mother's weakness for anything sweet by devilish means. But Martha and I were resolute. We refused to be charmed by the enticing confectionary he tried to force on us. It was hard, because we both had a sweet tooth and a constant craving, but we resisted, we didn't talk to him, just nodded or shook our heads, depending on what he asked us or offered us. We felt really sorry for the wily fox's wife—he could at least have waited with his fawning until after she was dead.

"That's what men are like," Mother said.

"Then I never want a man," I said.

"Don't imagine for a moment that women are any better," Mother said.

The sick woman died. Only a few days later, the widower was ringing our doorbell. He stood outside on the step with his arms full of flowers, but Mother didn't let him in. Martha and I listened from the door to the porch.

"I can't have men just turning up here whenever," she said. "You know that I'm married."

Following my short exercise routine in the bathroom, and without waking Martha, I went down for breakfast.

In reception, Ruth waved me into her office. She asked if we were comfortable in the room and happy with the hotel. And then, in a more intimate tone, she suggested that what I had seen, the thing with her and Dani, should be kept between them and me. And it might be wise not to mention anything to my sister. I agreed. It was not something I felt compelled to tell anyone. She thanked me, held the door open, and wished me a good day.

I found a table by the window. Once again, Martha took her time coming down and only appeared just before breakfast was over. Not that they seemed to be strict in the hotel, but Martha was indifferent to it all the same. And once again she asked if I could get some food for her. She felt so weak. She should perhaps get some different pills, as the ones she was taking didn't have any effect, she said. She expanded on how poorly she felt; even after hours of sleep she was still tired and lacking in energy. And the hotel seemed so dismal. And the other guests weren't particularly interested in any social interaction, not with us or with each other.

"The only ray of anything is that young man over there," Martha said.

She asked me if I'd noticed him. He had been sitting in the corner the day before, she said, and pointed with her knife. What did I think of him?

I drank the rest of my coffee, so I wouldn't need to answer.

"There's a dance here on Saturday," she said. "I hope he comes."

I pressed my finger down into the grinds, as though looking for a sign. I thought that if I were ever to tell the story of Martha and me, it could be a ghost story about two sisters, two irreconcilable and careworn sisters who wander the endless corridors of an old hotel for all eternity.

"Not to be vain, but I know that I'm quite good-looking," she said. "I've always been attractive to men."

For someone as weak and sickly as she claimed to be, Martha spoke with tireless enthusiasm. But then she stopped mid-sentence and looked up. She blushed. I turned around in my chair. Dani was standing there. She said it was nice to see me again.

I stood up and shook her hand.

"You must meet my sister," I said.

"I hope you slept well," Dani said, holding my gaze.

"Her name is Martha," I said.

Dani bowed to Martha. "Nice to meet you," she said.

It looked as though Martha wanted to say something, but not a sound came out.

Dani bowed again, then walked away.

I stood there, watching her, and only sat down once she'd left the room.

"What are your plans for today?" I asked Martha.

"Why didn't you say anything?" Martha said.

I didn't answer. I went to get more coffee.

On the wall above the buffet, there was a framed poster, an alluring and nostalgic picture of two skiers gliding effortlessly over a wide snowy slope, glittering in the sun. And across the blue sky, *Besuchen Sie das wunderbare Norwegen* was written in red letters. I had seen similar posters before, back when Father was dealing in antiques. He had bought the print from someone's estate. Apparently, it was valuable. Father was an eloquent rogue. I imagined him standing barefoot out in the back garden. He liked to work in daylight, and if the weather allowed it, he moved his entire workshop out onto the lawn. He had a solid oak table, and he would put his expensive treasure out on it for renovation. He patinated and repaired furniture, fixed crooked bureaus, an unsteady rococo chair, and he polished intricate candlesticks and cleaned fine porcelain.

Martha was clearly annoyed when I got back to the table.

"Are you trying to run away?" she said.

"I just wanted some more coffee," I said.

"Don't you realize how embarrassing the whole thing was for me?"

"What do you mean, embarrassing? You didn't say a word."

"Are you carrying on with that woman?"

"We said hello, and not much else, when I went down to get water for you last night."

"So she wanders around at night?"

I hesitated. I had to think of something. I needed to be creative, but I just hesitated even more.

"I can see it on you," Martha said.

"See what?"

"You're emanating guilt."

"She was thirsty as well," I explained, in a thin, hoarse voice.

"Yes, I'll bet she was thirsty," Martha said. "I know her type."

I couldn't be bothered to argue anymore. I put down my coffee cup and left. Martha followed. I could hear her footsteps behind me. I went up to our room and locked myself in the bathroom. Martha rapped on the door, a sharp, insistent knocking. I thought: What the hell's wrong with her? And what the hell's wrong with me? Why did I get so upset?

I heard Martha open the bottle of water, heard the bubbles rushing up. She swore. She turned on the TV. I lay down on the warm floor, rolled up one of the big towels, and put it under my head. It wasn't a comfortable position, but I fell asleep all the same. And I dreamt. I dreamt that I was dead. It was like I was playing a prank on those around me. I wanted to see if anyone would miss me. In my dream, I stormed out of life. I saw Father in the graveyard. He had thin clothes on, as usual. And there was Mother—lighting a cigarette. Martha was nowhere to be seen. The dream plumbed my depths. It was as though I was taking seismic measurements of myself. There was no sorrow or redemption in the dream, nor was there sorrow or redemption in waking up.

I got up from the hard tiles with a groan; I was stiff and had a headache. I listened at the door. The TV was still on in the room, I could hear dramatic music and gunshots. I opened the door in irritation. That was enough sulking for now.

Martha wasn't in the room. I called for her, but there was no answer. I then noticed that her suitcase was no longer there either. You could have knocked me over with a feather. The desperation of the one left behind knows no bounds, I thought. And what did this desperation entail? Nothing more heroic than that I felt that injustice had won. That Martha had tricked me. By resorting to such a demonstrative retreat, like childishly tossing your head when you can't admit that you've made a mistake, Martha would, if I knew her at all, repeat to herself that I had betrayed her, that I, her own sister, was scheming and disloyal, her rival in life. I tried to call her, to no avail. And my thoughts about her when I threw the phone down on the bed made me feel sick and dejected—it was a confounded mix of indignation and worry. The good qualities that were needed to endure the constant daily demands—consideration and respect—melted away into nothing in that bloody, fateful moment.

Martha didn't answer my phone calls. Martha didn't answer my text messages—they were concerned, they were desperate, I even apologized, but Martha remained silent. I tried to contain my bewilderment, tried to think rationally. Martha was no doubt at home. Where else would she go? It helped to imagine her on the train, still indignant and self-righteous, chin tilted, her suitcase in the rack. She'd probably asked some man to help her put it up there. Martha always had a trail of acolytes behind her. Those damn doe eyes.

I got dressed and went out. It was blowing outside, but the wind was surprisingly mild. It was as though the cold air was being pushed aside in great gusts. Once again, I trudged down toward the village. After half an hour, the wind died down and a fog rose up from the valley. I couldn't see anything and had to turn back. I stayed close to the snowbanks at the side of the road and hoped that no cars would come. It would be impossible to see me. The last time I'd gone for a walk, the snow squeaked underfoot, but now it was wet. Walking was heavy going. I felt the acute need to talk to someone—an urgent desire to say something nice. I hadn't thought about it before, but I wanted people to remember me well, should an accident befall me. I fumbled for my phone and leaned in toward a snowdrift. But who could I call? I was filled with a strange sensation. I couldn't remember anyone, not a soul. It was light, and then it got dark. I wanted to kiss the snow. No, I mustn't give in to grief. This was life. I needed happiness. Everyone needs happiness. And I had several joys in me. It wasn't easy to become who one wanted to be. There were so many wilful forces in a tired body. For example, there was my wild animal will, which refused to be tamed. And then there was my goodwill, which made me charming and sociable. And my unwillingness, I needed that. If I let go of my unwillingness, what then? I would be exploited, used for all kinds of errands and services. No, I had to make sure I didn't lose my truculence. We have to protect all our wills, I thought—we just need to deal with our destructive will and our weak will. It was no simple thing, striving to be a good person. I often said more than I wanted to say. And I regretted it and felt uneasy. It was as though I had lost the connection between my tongue and my brain.

I tried to get hold of Martha again. But she didn't answer this time either. I thought about leaving a message but couldn't think of anything sensible to say. She would see that I had called anyway and would know what it was about. If she had taken the train, she would be close to town by now. She would pull her suitcase toward the exit with a haughty look on her face, and then she would take a taxi home. How was the weather back home? Was it sleeting? Was there a thick fog there, too? It was as though an old grief inhabited me. It was impossible to escape. I felt the dampness of the rotting snow seep through my jacket. I had to get back to the hotel.

I had never doubted that my parents loved me. They were never reserved and seldom interfered with my choices. But now, lost in the low fog of the thaw, I longed for a mother who would order me straight home or a father who would say I should go untroubled to bed. Right now, I longed for someone who could whisper away my worries and dejection. What a poor, pathetic soul I was, like a contrary child.

When I got back to the hotel, Ruth was standing out on the steps. She'd been worried about me, she said. It was dangerous to be out in this fog. There were old mine shafts you could fall down, and anyone walking on the road could be mowed down by the snowplow. She led me through the reception, over to the big open fire, and helped me settle in one of the deep armchairs. She wanted to get me a drink, to make me a toddy with lots of sugar. I barely managed to nod. My teeth were chattering. But it didn't take long before the heat of the fire became unbearable. I stood up, pulled off my outer garments, loosened my scarf, and threw my hat on the floor. Ruth came in with her medicinal brew. I drank the hot liquid, handed the mug to her, and slumped back down in the chair.

"Can I sleep here?" I mumbled, curling up in a ball.

"Wouldn't you rather sleep in your bed?" Ruth said. "It's far more comfortable."

"Couldn't I lie down in there?" I said, and pointed toward the door behind the reception desk.

I remembered this much: there was a desk in there, and a bed.

Ruth was obliging once again. She let me rest in the backroom. And she closed the door quietly when she went out.

I lay down under the duvet. The bed linen smelled clean, like pine needles. I felt the fabric, ran it between my fingers. It was cool and slightly stiff. I lay without moving and studied all the captivating details in the room: a table lamp with a green lampshade, the packed bookshelf that covered an entire wall, and in the corner, in the shadows, in front of a large cupboard, a black wooden stepladder. The room had pink strié wallpaper up to a cornice with an intricate flower motif. There was something seductive about lying in the unfamiliar bed. It was like an easy journey to my inner depths. As though something still lingered over by the desk where Ruth and Dani had been standing, an outline of their bodies, a lighter patch. Even though I knew it was pure fantasy, I liked the thought. Had my eyes been playing tricks last night? No, I was not mistaken. I had not seen wrong. I hadn't dreamt or imagined any of it. The two women had stood there in such a tight embrace that they could have been one and the same being, like a perfectly balanced sculpture. I stared and stared at this mirage, this fixated image, which was no longer any more than a notion of lust. My own lust? Yes, it was also my own lust. And the desire? That I myself was standing there with Dani, with the young man, the young woman. That it was the two of us.

I heard footsteps, someone walking on the floor above, someone coming in from the direction of the kitchen and slamming a door, footsteps that made a noise, even on the carpeted floor of the corridor. How differently people walk, I thought. Here's someone who stomps, even though he's possibly both slim and faultless. And there were some light steps that I imagined was one of the impatient chambermaids. I lay listening as one often does when one finds oneself in an unfamiliar bed. There was someone with careful steps, impossible to identify, as though they were tiptoeing, like a thief moving around up there on the floor above. And then I heard Ruth's footsteps out in the reception. It had to be Ruth, I thought, and quickly put my hands on top of the duvet. Ruth's movements always seemed to have a purpose. Mother moved in the same way—as though she was on a mission, with something to do. And Father? Father had a firm, confident stride—his footsteps always gave me hope. As a child, I always brightened up before he even entered the room.

On a round bedside table, I found a crime novel, on top of a whole pile of books, with a title that caught my attention—*Death and the Maiden*. I leafed through it, and read: "And, strangely, something Lieutenant Trant had said to me just a little while ago trailed back into my thoughts. You can think you're in love when you're only really clinging to memories. You can fall out of love overnight. You can do almost anything—if you're young and you try hard enough. And I wondered...." I also found a German book in the pile. The title was *Verwirrung der Gefühle*, and it was written by Stefan Zweig. I opened it to a random page and whispered the words in an attempt to translate: "Before beginning, I leaf once again through the book which claims to depict my life. And once again I cannot help smiling. How did they think they could reach the true core of my being when they chose to approach it in the wrong way?"

I continued with this laborious endeavour for a while. I jumped back and forth in the book, read this section, then that, using my high school German as best I could. I was twenty-two years old. I had, of course, read a number of books before, but I had not read anything like this, that I related to with such pressing urgency. I was exhausted by all the concepts and all the images that leapt out of the text. But why had I chosen this book in particular? What was it in me that made me choose it? It didn't even have an attractive cover; in fact, it looked like all the other books in the pile. But nothing is entirely like something else: no two pillars in a church are ever identical, there is always a difference, and the same is true of two grapes, two leaves, two snowflakes— I always choose one rather than the other.

After about an hour, I put the book down and lay there, dozing, my mind filled with the images from what I had read. I only woke up when I heard Ruth talking to someone out in reception. I couldn't make out what was being said, only heard the different voices, and that she was talking to a man. The sound was muffled, as though they were mumbling to each other. If someone were to listen through the wall of our room, it would no doubt sound the same when Martha and I spoke to each other. But we'd squabble and bicker, so our voices would probably have a higher frequency. How do our endless discussions sound through the floor and walls? More and more often our conversations took a wrong turn. We were irritable, the slightest bagatelle became a conflict. And that awful argument at breakfast. What did Martha mean when she said I should have told her? What did this Dani have to do with us?

When we were younger, both Martha and I were more attentive, more considerate of each other. Once when we were at home alone for an entire week and had been given a generous amount of money for food, we went to the grocery and filled the shopping cart with pop and chips. Chips were one of our favourite things and, as we never had any in the house normally, we hoarded for the whole week. On the very first evening, we settled down in front of the TV and poured the golden potato chips into a huge glass bowl and placed it with great reverence between us. They crunched deliciously between our teeth, and we licked the salt from our fingers. We put as much as possible of the crunchy delight in our mouths—we stuffed our faces, to be honest. But then I noticed something stabbing my throat. At first, I thought it was just a small chip that had got stuck, but when Martha then held up three pins and said they were at the bottom of the bowl, I realized the gravity of the situation. I pointed to my throat. Martha thought on her feet and suggested that eating something cold would make the pin slip down more easily. She got some ice cubes and crammed them into my mouth. To no avail. We had to phone for help.

They photographed my digestive system at the hospital. The doctor showed me the X-rays. There were my intestines: my rectum, my colon, my small intestine, and there was my stomach, there was my esophagus—I had never realized it was so long. And the doctor pointed at the pin that was there inside me, white and shiny, with the small, round head pointing down.

They changed me and put me in a bed.

"She can't be alone," Martha said, and I still don't know how she did it, but Martha was also given hospital clothes and a bed to sleep in, right next to mine, and she stayed with me through the night. She was given the task of feeding me prunes until the pin came out by natural means.

My memories were interrupted by a knock, and before I could answer, the door swung open. It was Dani. She came right over to the bed, wanted to know if I was feeling better, and asked if I'd got the warmth back in my body. She seemed to look me up and down. It was unbearable to lie there like a sickly child. I sat up and said I felt fabulous.

She watched me as I pulled on my now-dry clothes. She asked if I wanted help.

"No," I said. "What would I need help with?"

It was a rude answer, but I was taken aback, couldn't think of anything better. What did she mean? Help to get dressed? I wasn't exactly on my last legs.

Following this little intermezzo, I went back to my own room, and as I unlocked the door, I hoped that Martha had come back, but she was still nowhere to be seen, and even though I was worried and increasingly angry, I made no further attempt to contact her. I got ready for bed and fell asleep as soon as my head hit the pillow.

In the morning, as I sat eating breakfast, it all became clear, this thing between me and Martha, something that might never have happened had it not been for my unexpected peace of mind, which was perhaps thanks to having read Zweig. Then and there, I relinquished any responsibility for Martha. It was self-assumed responsibility. I broke the pact, you might say. The undefined obligation. Who benefited from it anyway? Not Martha. Not me. In other words, I let it go. It was a decision that had crept up on me, uninvited and encouraging. From then on, I thought, I would respond differently to my surroundings.

The world was merciful that day, in a way I'd never before experienced. No demands were made. I felt no degrading or wretched shame.

I stood in the doorway to the ballroom, where Saturday's dance was going to take place, and watched a carpenter who was replacing some of the floorboards. I watched him without discretion. Like an overgrown schoolgirl, I leaned against the door frame with my arms akimbo and followed his every move, as if I were his apprentice—a pleasing thought. And when he turned around and said hello, I was neither embarrassed nor shy. I walked into the room and shook his hand. I told him my name, surname included. Without thinking, I said how nice it was to watch him work. I said the sound of carpentry was like music. I said I envied him, I envied the hammer and the saw, the spirit level and drill. I chatted away about the wood that the carpenter was fitting, about the sharp-edged peace of the planks. And before I pulled myself away, I said I wished we were somehow related.

Fortunately, it seemed that the carpenter, a lean, older man, was not put out by my rambling, as he continued to work with skill and focus.

Goodness. In retrospect, I think the man must have thought I was mad. But at the time, it never occurred to me. In the moment, I felt elated by my newly acquired inner peace, by my decision to be frank, by Zweig, by who knows what. Also, in retrospect, I have planted a seed of doubt as to whether it really was a state of inner peace, or if I, for a short while, had been bestowed a fleeting but nonetheless gratifying fervour, a much-needed confidence.

On the way back to my room, I was stopped by Ruth. She put her hand gently on my shoulder, as though she were afraid I might break, or perhaps she was so careful because I was obviously lost in my own thoughts. She apologized for the hammering and hoped the noise wasn't disturbing. It would be a day or two before it was finished, she said, and our room was directly above the ballroom, so we would, of course, be compensated for the inconvenience.

"Where was Martha yesterday, by the way?" Ruth asked.

The question came completely out of the blue and my response was brief. I said that I was not responsible for my sister.

In the evening, I ate a three-course meal and got drunk. It wasn't particularly obvious, I'm fairly certain of that, as alcohol actually makes me less talkative, more introverted. I sat peaceful and happy on my own at the table and did not plague anyone with pointless chatter. I didn't want to give myself away, I wasn't going to bother others with unwanted attention.

An older man, who had apparently lived in the hotel for twelve years, had his own table over by the door. He gave me a gallant nod, and I nodded in return. For a moment I was tempted to ask if he wanted company, but then couldn't bring myself to do it, all the same. We raised our glasses to each other a couple of times. I decided to call him Apollo.

The snow was falling thick and fast outside. I liked the honesty with which the snowflakes settled on the landscape. I liked the feeling of being suspended in a dream. My movements slowed. I felt an almost friendly affection for the other guests, the families and couples seated around beautifully lit tables. They smiled and chatted, with an almost naive trust in words; they maintained the illusion that they were understood through the quiet, pleasant hum of voices. I sat there with a sense of spine-tingling, surging alertness. I feared nothing, I had no enemies. My offering was an open, accommodating silence. Ruth came over to my table and poured me a cup of coffee.

"That'll put hairs on your chest," she whispered in my ear.

"That's how I like it," I said.

"I know," she said.

When I took a sip, I burned my tongue, so I cooled it with a teaspoon. It undoubtedly looked rather odd. The large, round lamps hung from the ceiling like moons. It felt like I was alone on some unknown celestial body, a glowing satellite, despite the other guests, and even though Ruth was so attentively present.

That night, I dreamt that the snow had gone. The birds twittered as though possessed, and the beds in front of the hotel were full of crocuses and lilies of the valley. Spring overwhelmed me, it was too beautiful—in truth, alarming. I got it into my head that the ground would give way, that soon everything would be swallowed up. Would we continue after death? Would we still be ourselves? A white cat stalked across the small patch of gravel up by the chapel. I was filled with despair in my dream. I had no resistance, no way to protect myself. It was as though everything around me was about to fall apart, my pores lost their breath, my muscles felt stiff, my mind was foggy. Strong currents pushed against me. Nothing in me felt solid. In the coffee grinds at the bottom of a cup, I saw a bear, a fish, a herd of goats in the shade of an enormous pine tree.

On Friday afternoon, a convoy of cars snaked up the mountainside from the valley. I stood naked at the window, a towel turbaned round my head, and watched the beams from the headlights twist and turn in the dark. It was as though there was a cluster of will-o'-the-wisps down there, looking for people to lead astray. The weekend guests were arriving. I looked forward to seeing new people. Martha and I were similar in that. She also loved to be among strangers; being with people with no obligation unleashed her otherwise tethered curiosity. I missed her now. She would have appreciated this sudden influx of guests. The dining room and reception would be a lot livelier. We both liked to live cheek by jowl with people—polite exchanges by the buffet, postcards that were studied, remarks that were made, all the languages—there was solace in it. If Martha had appeared now, if she had spoken to me as though there were no differences between us, she would no doubt have told me that she was looking forward to breakfast, to dinner, and that she felt very continental, like a seasoned traveller, like an adventurer. But what about me? What would I say? Would I chide her or act as though nothing had happened?

I normally prefer to keep quiet. When my tongue loosened, there was a danger that my voice would start to glow with enthusiasm, and before I knew it, I sounded like an excited child. And on the occasions that I said too much, the times when I wasn't careful, all meaning disappeared, and my insight seemed to go under cover. And if I didn't pay attention, my judgment could fail me, and I became an obliging fool. I can't remember when I became so self-conscious, when this unbearable and bombastic attitude took possession of me. I liked to be amenable, liked to make others feel comfortable. I wasn't exactly servile. But Mother noticed that I had changed.

"What's wrong with you?" she asked. "What's wrong with you, Ella?"

And my orgasms changed, they didn't tear through my body like before. They were quieter, longer, almost like they were in slow motion. I calmed down, wasn't as anxious as before, not so easy to rile. I found myself thinking I was lucky, that I was favoured from above.

And many years later, abandoned in a hotel room, I thought it was inconceivable what we do to each other, what we do to ourselves.

I decided to go down for a drink. I needed something warm and invigorating. Two men were sitting at the bar. They were talking together as though conspiring about something secret, but when I wriggled up onto one of the high stools, they raised their whisky glasses, swirling the ice cubes. I gave them a brief smile, then turned the stool so I had my back to them. It wasn't meant as a rejection, but rather that I couldn't bear the thought of getting stuck in one of those boring conversations. It was one of the paradoxes that Martha and I shared. I liked it when there were other people at the bar, even being caught up in a crush, but I couldn't be bothered to talk to anyone, to converse.

And the bartender was none other than Dani. Once again, she asked how I was, and again she scrutinized me.

"Is it possible to have an Irish coffee?" I asked.

"Of course," she said. "Do you like it sweet?"

"Yes," I said. "I like it sweet."

She suggested I try one with aquavit, as it tasted like caramel.

Without waiting for an answer, she made up the drink. She topped it with a squirt of cream, put in a straw, and slid the concoction over to me.

I drank it quickly and ordered another.

More guests appeared. A group of young people settled down around a table. Dani didn't chat or humour them, but she was friendly, and quickly found out what they wanted.

It felt fantastic to sit there and drink myself into a stupor. I ordered yet another drink, felt tipsy, in a good mood. The trees outside were golden. From where I was sitting, the entire hotel appeared to be made of glass, and outside were mountains of gold, liquid gold that covered all the peaks and outcrops and gorges. It was snowing gold—gold dust danced on the wind. And then, through this glittering membrane, this sheer pleasure, I noticed a vibration in my bag. It was Martha calling. I hesitated at first. Was unsure. Afraid of losing this sorely needed balance. But I had to hear what was on her mind. After all, no matter how I felt, I was obliged to acknowledge my sister when she finally gave a sign of life. I answered simply by saying her name, and, as though we had our own code, she said mine.

"I'm sorry," she said. "I'll be back at the hotel tomorrow."

"That's good," I said.

"It takes time to understand," she said.

"Yes," I said.

"Well, see you then."

"See you."

Nothing more.

That was it.

I grabbed my glass. I remembered something Mother used to say, something like the sick only want one thing, whereas the rest of us want so much, all the time.

When the other guests in the bar started to leave, Dani kept me back. She felt like a schnapps, now that they were closed, and wanted me to keep her company. She tidied and wiped down the tables and counter. Together we carried the glasses out into the kitchen, and Dani put the dishwasher on.

The moon was shining in through the big windows. I was struck by how delicate Dani was, like a youth in an old English film.

She opened the enormous fridge and took out a bottle of gin.

"I like women who drink," she said. "There's something effortless about them that only comes out with alcohol."

She held the bottle out to me, and when I waved it away, she grabbed me by the waist and forced me to take a swig. I didn't give in. It was below my dignity. And Dani realized she'd gone too far. She put the bottle down. At that very moment, the light went on and Ruth was standing in the doorway.

"I was helping Dani tidy up," I said.

It was a sorry excuse, but Ruth didn't seem to be suspicious anyway. She thanked me and said we could just help ourselves to some food. There were open sandwiches in the cold room. She was about to go to bed, as she had to get up early, and it was already late. She stroked Dani's neck and then said goodnight.

I listened, heard a faint creaking as she climbed the stairs. And then Dani was up close. She looked me in the eyes. She didn't need to ask now. I wanted what she wanted. I pressed myself against her, managed to knock my forehead against hers by mistake, and the impact hurt. We kissed. Dani was good. I felt unwell and euphoric at the same time. Everything around me withered, everything around me blossomed. The world reeled. And even though in the moment I felt a pang of loss for all that I'd had, and all that was gone, it was so easy, it was so easy to be enchanted.

I TRY
TO DESCRIBE
THE SUDDEN
DESIRE

"I want it to be a soft green, not as blue-green as a robin's egg, but not as yellow-green as daffodil buds. Now, the only sample I could get is a little too yellow, but don't let whoever does it go to the other extreme and get it too blue. It should just be a sort of greyish yellow-green. Now, the dining room. I'd like yellow. Not just yellow, a very gay yellow. Something bright and sunshiny. I tell you, Mr. PeDelford, if you'll send one of your men to the grocery for a pound of their best butter and match that exactly, you can't go wrong! Now, this is the paper we're going to use in the hall. It's flowered, but I don't want the ceiling to match any of the colours of the flowers. There are some little dots in the background, and it's these dots I want you to match. Not the little greenish dot near the hollyhock leaf, but the little bluish dot between the rosebud and the delphinium blossom. Is that clear? Now, the kitchen is to be white. Not a cold, antiseptic hospital white. A little warmer, but not to suggest any other colour but white. Now for the powder room—in here. I want you to match this thread, and don't lose it. It's the only spool I have, and I had an awful time finding it! As you can see, it's practically apple red. Somewhere between a healthy Winesap and an unripened Jonathan."

DESIRE
MINUS
HAPPINESS

Saturday morning. I woke with a gasp, and in the dark it took me a while to understand that I was back in my room. I was alone in bed. Dani must have crept out; I hadn't even noticed, which was strange, as I was a light sleeper. It was as though time was out of joint. How long had the late-night visitation lasted? I had been so full of desire, so filled with something pure and irrepressibly blissful. And Dani's rough wantonness had not bothered or pained me in the least. Quite the opposite, in fact—it gave exceptional scope for pleasure. But now, abandoned in the large hotel bed, I saw myself as a kind of spectator, a random witness to what had happened, and it struck me that this detachment, the fact that I hadn't managed to fully grasp what had happened, no matter how intense, bothered me in a very diffuse way and made me feel ashamed.

I fumbled for the switch, but as soon as the light exploded in my eyes, I changed my mind and turned it off again. I went over to the window and slowly opened the curtains. The morning blush was a kind of release, the sky full of pale pink cupid clouds.

It dawned on me that I had dreamt about Father. We were in a garden covered in snow. Me and him. There were garlands of lights in the frozen fruit trees.

"What time does your watch say?" I asked.

"Which watch?" he asked.

I rested my head against his chest. I was as still as a doe that has run over the fields.

"Enjoy the war," he said. "Peace will be intolerable."

Oh, rapture. Oh, mercy. And the silence, the silence in the dream was like a friendly arrow, it was like justice—expansive, navigable, and supreme.

These fragments from my dream cleared my head. I stripped off the duvet cover and pillowcases, pulled off the sheet, then threw them all in a pile on the floor. Martha would be back soon and she mustn't suspect anything, not at any cost, least of all that someone had slept in her bed. I wanted the room to be perfect when she returned. It was perhaps a little excessive, but I decided to take the bus down into the village to buy flowers—Martha loved flowers. I remembered the candyfloss-pink tulips she had bought with her first paycheque from the perfumery. She chose the best vase, but then forgot to fill it with water, and already the next day, the flowers hung their heads, exhausted, toward the table. Like dead women. Why did I think they were women?

I skipped breakfast, snuck out the back and down the fire escape. I didn't want to meet either Dani or Ruth. I was just in time for the bus that connected with the morning train. I knew the timetable by heart, I could remember things like that without any effort.

I was the only person to get on. The driver said the roads were icy. He said I didn't need to pay. I thanked him and sat down at the front, so I could get the best view of the valley.

Once I was down in the small centre, it only took a few minutes to do what I had come to do. I picked out some fresh tulips in the flower shop and asked the florist to wrap the generous bunch in tissue paper and newspaper.

On the way back to the bus stop, I walked past the park. A gaggle of children were skating on the frozen pond. It wasn't a large surface of ice, but they shrieked with delight at their sudden, unsteady movements. And while I stood there watching their carefree game, I became aware of a woman in uniform standing beside me: she had materialized without me noticing. Or had she snuck up on me? At first I thought she was from the police, and wondered if it was illegal to skate in the park, but when I looked at her, which seemed necessary as she was standing so close, I saw that she was a Salvation Army soldier. She said hello and didn't I think it was wonderful to see the children play?

"Yes," I said. "Yes, of course, it's wonderful."

"That is how God speaks to us," she said.

You could see her breath when she spoke. And without me having asked, and without warning, she started to talk about all the terrible feelings we humans harbour in our hearts.

"Sin is just around the corner in every home, in every soul," she said.

Before I managed to tear myself away, she started to tell me about the prophecies in the Bible, that Judgement Day was nigh. But we need not despair, for the Holy Spirit would come to those who believed.

I tried to stem the flow of words. Of all things, I asked her what she was called, and that made her stop. She studied me as though considering whether or not to give me such confidential information.

"Aud," she said, eventually. "And you? What's your name?"

"I'm staying up at the hotel," I said. "I just popped down to buy some flowers."

I held out the large paper bag of well-wrapped tulips.

"We must keep watch every night," she said. "Dark forces are at play. There will be a terrible storm."

Even though I could tell the woman was a little unhinged, I felt a strange sympathy. Who did she remind me of? No one. It was fascinating to realize that I'd never met such an eccentric soul before. She both entertained and unsettled me, and I almost allowed myself to be seduced by her overblown ramblings. I dismissed any objections and gave her a hug. She smelled of alcohol, and the sweetness on her breath gave her a kind of poetic sensibility.

"I have to hurry," I said.

She stood as though turned to stone.

"I have to hurry," I said again.

"I feel so indescribably tired," she said. "So tired that even the thought of trimming flowers and putting them in a vase exhausts me."

"I have to catch the bus," I said.

"Thank you," she said.

There was no one else on the bus now either, and once again, the driver refused to let me pay.

I sat at the back, turned around in my seat to catch a final glimpse of Aud, but she was nowhere to be seen. The children skated round and round on the ice, the snow-clad trees stood around the pond, and the Salvation Army soldier had simply evaporated.

When we were little girls, Martha and I had a bird, a cockatiel, and it imitated everything it heard; it imitated us, it imitated the voices on the radio, it even imitated the washing machine. Mother said it was like having a crazy child in the house. On the few occasions that we asked her why she hadn't had more children, she said it wasn't possible to endure such pain more than twice in life—it was nature's way of ensuring that people controlled themselves. She believed that women who had more than two children were unbalanced—yes, she truly believed they had no control.

When I got back to the hotel, the chambermaid had been in and tidied the room. She had vacuumed and aired, and the bed linen was smooth and fresh—no trace of the night's deceitful delights. A thought struck me: what if Dani liked to tell Ruth about her seductions? And what if Ruth was turned on by the titillating and intimate details of Dani's conquests?

What then?

I had no reason to berate myself.

Or did I?

Minimum pain, maximum pleasure, as my father used to say. But whether he was simply reminding himself of this hedonistic maxim, or he merely saw it as part of our education, was hard to know.

I went into the bathroom, put the plug in the bath, and turned on the taps. And when I lowered myself into the warm water, I thought it was time to kick some old habits. From now on I would be bolder and, if possible, more clear-sighted. I would show any demons from the past the door. I would make my soul sing; no longer would it be useless and disempowered. My soul was, in fact, wiser than me. I wanted to protect it from all that was dismal. From now on, it would not have to deal with my desperation, my constant worries. No more would it be left to wallow in wild imaginings. I thought about Dani. And reluctantly fantasized about her. She put a hand under my chin and leaned in over me, bit my lower lip—it hurt, it turned me on. I came quickly, my orgasm hard, almost painful.

I CONDEMN
MY PATHETIC
HEART
AND SOUL

Martha had managed to convince Father to drive her all the way up to the hotel. Or perhaps I was wrong. Perhaps Father was the one who suggested it. He loved going wherever the wind blew or visiting places where he'd heard there was a grand old bureau, a rustic writing desk, or some antique decorations.

As children, there were times when Martha and I were allowed to join him on these excursions. We learned early on that we mustn't disturb him while he was haggling. It was one of the few things that could irritate him. One summer afternoon, we were with him in a crammed second-hand shop out in the country. He was interested in a painting and a rocking cradle that was decorated with traditional patterns. He had spoken warmly about these objects when we were in the car, but in the shop, he wrinkled his nose and just wandered around, inspecting all manner of clutter and junk.

When, after a great deal of toing and froing, he took the cradle and the painting to the counter to pay, he noted nonchalantly: "So it was five hundred kroner for the painting and eight hundred for the cradle?"

"That's right," the antique dealer said.

Father pulled a wad of notes from his inside pocket. "That'll be twelve hundred," he said.

"No, it's thirteen hundred," the antique dealer said.

"Sorry, I'm so bad at mental arithmetic," Father said.

"So you could just as well have said fourteen hundred?"

"No," Father said, winking at me and Martha. "I'm not that bad."

I was reading on the sofa when Father and Martha came. I heard the key in the door and shot up, looking quickly around to see if any of Dani's things were still there. But, of course, there was nothing there that could betray her visit.

"Lovely, you've bought tulips," was the first thing Martha said when she came into the room. She hugged me sincerely, holding me while Father set down her bags and waited. When she finally released me from this overwhelming embrace, Father grabbed me around the waist and lifted me up.

"You look good," he said. "You're as light as a feather."

"It's because my hair is all gone," I said.

Father put me down and ran his hand carefully over my head. He started to wander about, as he tended to do, with his hands behind his back. He went from room to room and from one piece of furniture to the next, turned a chair round, examined the base of a lamp, lifted a bowl.

"Isn't it grand here?" he said, pointing at the stucco on the ceiling and the headboard with the neat carvings. "Not bad. Not bad at all. Is the food good as well?"

I hastened to state that I thought we should find a place to eat down in the village.

Martha looked curiously at me. "Why?" she asked. "They have a wonderful menu here in the hotel."

I hadn't prepared a good explanation. It was just a desperate attempt to avoid bumping into Dani or Ruth. I needed time. I was afraid I would make everything known with just one wrong breath. It was only now I realized that what Dani had set in motion was a betrayal of Ruth and that I had recklessly allowed myself to be pulled into it. Not for one moment had it crossed my mind to ask Dani if Ruth was aware of our nighttime adventure, if the two of them had an open relationship, or if there was an agreement between them, a trust that Dani had broken.

No, of course Ruth didn't know about it, I thought. Of course it was a betrayal.

I came out with something about the staff no doubt being busy preparing for the event that evening, and fortunately Martha agreed. In any case, we could both do with some air before the party. We'd be able to grab a bite so long as we didn't linger.

For the second time that day, I was on my way down the winding road. Martha sat in front, beside Father. She got carsick so quickly. I leaned in between the seats and asked Father how Mother was. She had got it into her head that she wanted to go to Japan, he told us. She wanted to visit the Ama women. She wanted to learn to dive for pearls.

Father kept a straight face as he came out with this peculiar information. I poked him on the back of the neck and said he was lying.

They had a strange relationship, Mother and Father. They hardly spoke at home, especially not to each other. Even as a child I had understood that a shadow rested between them, a vague, ever-present shadow that separated them from each other. Once, I heard Father say he would have given his life to get Mother. It was a mysterious declaration.

"Oh, life is way too much," Mother had replied. "Give me some peace of mind instead."

The only place to eat that was open in the village was a roadside café. Martha and Father each ordered a cheeseburger. I settled for a milkshake and a salad.

I didn't say much, but it was good to be in their company. Father seemed so young, sitting there with cheeseburger.

"I've noticed something strange while I've been travelling around," he said. "When it comes to women, it seems as though men in one country always think that men in another country are luckier than them. For example, Italian men like Swiss women. German men rate Spanish women the highest. And men from Greece, they love Nordic women. Yes, that's how it is across the board, no exceptions."

Martha laughed at Father's comment. She was shining, her radiance almost stretching out toward me, and she repeated that short hair really suited me.

Martha. Martha, with her divine, seductive features. Martha, with her voice like a burbling stream. For weeks she had behaved as though she were the only person to have ever had a nervous breakdown. She had disturbed me. She had devastated me. I thought I couldn't stand her. I wanted to distance myself from her, to protect myself. Why couldn't I do it? Because I was afraid of her? Because I loved her? The thought scared me. But now, she was both devoted and trusting. Nothing threatened us. I was tempted to suggest that Father could stay at the hotel for a couple of nights. It would do him good, I was sure of it. But then the spell was broken. Father checked his watch and devoured the rest of the burger. He really had to get going.

Even though he was in a rush, he insisted on driving us back up to the hotel. I didn't say a word during the journey. Father gave us a brief lecture on mining, while Martha sat and whistled.

When we swung in by the main entrance, the newly cleared parking area was packed with cars.

"Where there is dancing, there are people," Father said. "That's how it is, out here in the provinces."

We hugged him before getting out of the car. Martha first, then me, a little awkwardly over the seatback.

Before driving off, he rolled down the window and shouted to us: "I'm all for shenanigans, but with the right people. Remember that, girls. Remember that."

We stood there and waved until the car disappeared behind the large mounds of snow that had been pushed to the side of the road's sharp bend. To my astonishment, Martha grabbed my hand and led me. It took me so much by surprise that I didn't even consider tearing myself away. Even when we walked past the reception, I let her keep hold of me. I caught a glimpse of Ruth behind the desk. She was busy welcoming some guests who had just arrived. Her eyes darted up. I tried to smile at her but only managed to grimace, thinking my face must have looked like an Asiatic demon mask.

I stopped in the middle of the stairs and pulled my hand toward me. I had lost control. And I hated it. But Martha didn't seem to notice my irritation. She pointed at a portrait, commenting on the jaunty bonnet the young woman had on her head.

"I'm looking forward to the party," she said. "I've brought three new outfits with me. You have to help me choose."

I didn't reply.

Outside the door to our room, Martha stopped and grabbed my hand again. "Thank you for being so charitable," she said.

Charitable? I thought. Where had that word come from? And where had her sudden mildness come from? I had acknowledged, with relief, that I wasn't responsible for Martha. There were no longer any oppressive obligations between us. But I was responsible for myself, and now I just wanted to sleep, lie down, close my eyes, and disappear. All of my bold decisions had disintegrated. I touched my head. Had my hair turned grey? It felt so lifeless. And my eyes? Were they yellow? Of course, I knew they weren't yellow. They were no more yellow than the sky. No more yellow than the glass-like surface of the mountainside. But still. Those yellow eyes. That yellow sky. That yellow snow.

I was more predisposed to drama than I wanted to admit. The thin air up at this altitude had made me childish and unpredictable. I realized I was going to have to fight hard battles in this place. It was a fundamental truth. Or was it Martha's sudden generosity that had unnerved me?

I let us in.

"It's wonderful to be back," Martha said. She opened the sliding doors to the bedroom and, in one movement, leapt onto the bed.

I stood looking at her.

"What's up?"

I hesitated.

"What's up?"

"Nothing," I said.

"You have a nosebleed," Martha said.

I wiped my nose with the back of my hand. I really did have a nosebleed, which was unusual for me. I found a tissue in my handbag, sat on the couch, tipped my head back, and stuffed a rolled-up strip up my nostril. Everything flickered toward me in a peculiar way as I sat there with my throat tensed. I realized that I had been chasing life all these years, or, more precisely, that life had been running away from me. I was full of emotions I couldn't stand. And, as if it were the moment of my death—yes, I was predisposed to drama at the time—I pictured Mother, raking leaves in the garden. I was seven years old. I thought we worked well together, Mother and me.

I stood on my toes, lifted one arm, and let my index finger glide along the hem of her jacket. She leaned forward so I could sniff her hair. Mother smelled like apples and rain and mint. A cloud moved over the sun, narrowing the light.

"Surely it's stopped bleeding now?" Martha said.

I removed the paper carefully. The blood had dried. It looked black.

"We have to get ready for the party," she said.

She took garment after garment from the suitcase: a shimmering gold dress, a pink silk blouse and a red skirt, several pairs of high heels.

I went to the bathroom, tried to flush the bloody paper down the toilet, but it bobbed up again like a fishing float. The water turned red.

Martha came in after me. It wasn't possible to hold her back.

"Remember that time we won five hundred kroner on that scratch card you had?" she asked. "Remember we spent it all on sweets?"

I flushed the toilet again, and the water rushed out from the cistern. I looked down into the toilet bowl. The bloody mess had finally disappeared.

While she continued trying on clothes, Martha reminisced about our childhood and our mutual love of treats. Did I remember how we used to eat loads of banana chocolate? How we would take huge handfuls and chomp until we drooled? And yes, I remembered. I remembered the luminescent jelly babies we stuffed into our mouths. It was like we were both crazy. But when the nauseating sugar rush reached the muscles in our hearts, it was as if everything inside us was vibrating, and the trembling was almost unbearable.

"What do you think of this?" Martha said, twirling round in the tight gold dress.

"You look lovely," I said.

"Aren't you going to change?" Martha asked. "Time is marching on."

"Is it okay if I shower first?" I asked.

"Just leave some hot water for me," Martha said.

I was quick. It felt wonderful to lather shampoo into my short hair. There was something calming about being able to feel the shape of my head so distinctly. I rinsed myself with cold water. And after I had towelled myself dry and warm, I pulled on a pair of grey woollen bell-bottoms and a petroleum-green polo neck.

Martha studied me, placing herself in front of me and frowning, like a model scout. And I knew what was coming. Now came the criticisms. Now came the small, subtle remarks I hated protesting against. But no—she just told me I looked smart. I was so perplexed. I took a peach from the fruit bowl. I had always believed it was important to keep a certain distance from compliments like that, flattery that aligned with one's nature, but now I was happy, even though I wasn't sure if Martha meant I actually looked intelligent or if I just looked fashionable in this outfit. One was possibly as good as the other. Surely it wasn't the case that my sister and I suspected each other of betrayal all the time?

"What are you eating?" Martha asked.

"A peach," I replied.

"But aren't you allergic to peaches?"

"Perhaps my body has changed," I said.

I know that a genuine and perpetual acquiescence provides us with the most reasonable and resilient connection to other people. This is the case when we meet people fleetingly on the bus, in the shop, or at the market, and not least in our relationship with our nearest and dearest. When it comes to me and my sister, for example, a crumb of humility would easily have prevented us from ending up in this never-ending and infantile cycle of bickering that has characterized our relationship since the end of our teenage years. I believe that's when it started, this cold juddering between us, this unhappiness. Whether it was my fault or hers, I don't know. Well, I suppose *fault* isn't really the right word. Maybe that's how it is for everyone? Childhood is over, adolescence is nearing its end, and this childlike approach to the world is lost—this naive connection to Mother and Father and siblings ceases to exist. And Martha and I were almost the same age, which resulted in this fracturing, this loss, starting almost simultaneously.

Yes, it was a loss, a warmth that diminished completely unexpectedly. Did it start in a rather simple way, with a comment? Something that in itself was meant innocently? I don't know. But I can picture Martha in the living room back home, removing wilted flowers from a vase. I asked her about something, or I said something unintentional, I can't remember what, but regardless of whether it was a question in good faith or a thoughtless comment, Martha stiffened, like a frightened bird. She is a bird, I thought. And then she started to speak, and what she said was tangled and incoherent. It was like there was no warmth in her, no genuine sincerity. Even her agitation seemed like nothing but a role, something with which she postulated and flirted. I'd never seen her like that before. Now it was like she had drifted away from me. There wasn't even any real curiosity in her voice when she asked me what I'd meant by the verbal sting I'd come out with. And what followed this episode were woeful days and sleepless nights. After a week, I was thoroughly tired of her. I was drained. I hated her grating voice. It forced me into exhaustion and resentment. With clear suspicion, we tried to expose the slightest sign of weakness in each other. We both tried to expose the other's flaws and vulnerabilities. For a while I thought it would end, that it was just a phase, that the bottomlessness I felt would change shape. For a long time, I kind of believed we would be reconciled. But that optimism also disappeared completely, and I understood that nothing would be the same as it had been before.

Only once during the period that stretched from that moment in the living room, Martha with the wilting flowers—what a telling picture—to when we found ourselves in the alpine village, in the glass hotel, can I remember Martha and me finding our way back to that closeness, that compassion we'd taken for granted when we were younger, and it was the day she left— that is, before I knew anything about the plans she had. I'd injured myself during a lawn mower demonstration in the shop where I worked. It wasn't serious, but it hurt, and when I came home, the provisional bandage I'd wrapped around my hand was soaked through with blood. As soon as Martha saw it, she helped me treat the wound. We each sat on a kitchen stool. Martha carefully washed away the congealed blood and attentively applied a new bandage. I was moved. I stroked her back. She was left-handed. Why did I think that was significant? But when we both stood up and I thanked her, she pulled away. It was as though she'd regretted what she'd done.

Oh, how I missed being a child as I sat there on the stool, my wound dressed. I remember so well how, on summer evenings just before we went to bed, Martha and I would turn off all the lights in the room before pulling off our trousers and tops. It was a procedure we'd taught ourselves to prevent insects, seduced by the lamps, from entering the room—both Martha and I were extremely sensitive to all types of stings and bites.

Oh, how I missed that time, when we, like small, blind girls, learned to deal with our lot in life, fumbling for the window latches to let in the crisp night air.

IF I DIDN'T
HAVE A
CRIMINAL MIND,
I WOULDN'T
SOLVE
THE MYSTERY

The orchestra that was hesitantly starting to play consisted of three lean men in their early thirties and a waif-like, thinly dressed woman. She couldn't have been much older than twenty, but had a surprisingly deep voice that suited the typical songs they were warming up with.

Martha danced with a man from the village for a long time. He'd seemed so determined when he came over to us. He held out his hand and told us his name, and Martha nodded and said yes before he'd actually asked her if she wanted to dance. He was wearing a black suit and pointed blue shoes. It was unsettling.

I remained standing against the wall, that classic image of sadness, but there was nothing sorrowful about the state I was in. I had a glass of whisky in one hand and a pint in the other. I respectfully declined those who came courting—I wasn't dancing because I'd hurt my ankle, I said.

I drank myself tipsy. I hadn't had such a good time in ages.

Later on, during a small break, I caught sight of the slender songstress in the hustle and bustle in front of the bar and was tempted to find a shawl to throw over her shoulders. I take after Mother. I can't stand seeing people freeze, but I restrained myself, not giving in to the impulse. My God, what was I thinking? She was a complete stranger, she might feel uncomfortable, or even offended.

Martha came over to me, breathless and in high spirits. She wanted to buy me a drink. That is, she would pay if I went and got them. She couldn't be bothered with all the jostling at the bar.

My sister didn't care about thinking, couldn't be bothered to keep her senses sharpened. And now she was standing there, warm and elated after dancing, revealing two sides of her soul at the same time: she was generous and she was lazy. But I didn't want to get into a discussion. I took the note she gave me—it was warm, too—and then went to the bar to order two Aperols.

While I was waiting for the drinks, I caught sight of Dani over by the door. She was flirtatiously greeting two women. I was sure she'd seen me, but she took her time. She seemed so untroubled, so at home in herself, in her own skin.

Martha carefully sipped the orange drink. I finished mine in a few large gulps and put the empty glass on the windowsill.

"He's so incredibly nice," Martha said.

I looked past her. Dani was coming toward us. It was as though I was preparing myself for a secret and much-welcomed reunion. It was a peculiar realization— like consciously allowing oneself to be uninhibited, almost in love.

"He's invited me to go with him to Lichtenstein," Martha continued. "He has an amazing flat there. By the sea, I think."

"Oh," I said. "Lichtenstein? By the sea?"

"I don't know," Martha said. "I've never been to Lichtenstein."

I kept quiet.

"I never thought this would happen to me," Martha said. "Meeting such an amazing man."

Dani gave me a hug, kissed me on the cheek, and said a quick hello to Martha.

"Aren't you dancing?" she asked.

"I've been dancing all evening," Martha said.

Dani looked at me. "What about you?"

I didn't get the chance to reply before Martha announced that she didn't have much time.

"We're leaving before it gets too late," she said.

She said "we" as though there was talk of certainty, a long-term relationship, a marriage. And she said "too late" as though this was her last chance.

"Are you both leaving?" Dani said.

"No, Ella is staying here," Martha said. "I'm the one who has plans."

Martha hugged me as well.

"Thanks," she said, then left.

For a moment, I was half a person, yes, I really felt like I'd been halved, an incomplete figure. From where I stood, everything was suddenly inextricably linked to itself, to its own reflection: the hall; the music, which was starting up again; the people dancing and jostling and clamouring loudly. Everything and everyone kept their own unstable, frozen form. And Dani—even her friendly gestures and flattering words were ominous now.

Almost in a daze, I agreed to dance. Dani pulled me tightly against her, and even though the song was rather frenzied, she led me in a series of slow movements. But I was already tired of the party. I wanted to go and rest, to be in peace.

"Sorry," I said, with no further explanation, before abandoning her on the dance floor.

When I got to the room, Martha was packing. I lay down on the bed and asked her to turn off the light when she left.

"I hope you're not sad," she said.

"I'm not sad," I said.

She carried her luggage into the corridor, turned off the light, and remained standing in the doorway. "It would be nice to know that you're happy for me," she said.

"I'm happy for you," I said.

"It's just that you don't sound particularly happy."

"I am happy," I said.

Martha waved at me. Her silhouette was black and sharp. I felt a pang of self-loathing because it was as though I was bidding a stranger farewell. So little remained between us—only numb restlessness, no joy, only strife. Everything was over. It was gone, all of it. It was done.

When the door clicked shut, I lay and looked at an outline, some kind of optical impression on my retina, a remembered figure. It was like looking at a faraway cloud, waiting for a storm. But no storm came. Neither snow nor rain came. No powerful gusts of wind came. Nothing revealed itself apart from the darkness in the room and the silence in my heart.

I wasn't sure whether it was the alcohol or Martha's retreat that had made me so melancholy.

"Who are you?" I whispered to myself.

"I don't know," I replied.

And Martha? She was a muttonhead. All of these compliments that, with the greatest ease, fuelled the most pathetic parts of her. Considering I'd always regarded her as intelligent, yes, at times extremely intelligent, it was unbelievable to observe these charlatans she fell for—men whose shoes were too shiny—and how they, with overinflated praise and ingratiating admiration, gained access to Martha's brain and will. These idiots could be both unenlightened and cunning, but they always had something to offer, something Martha claimed she had always longed for: a night at the opera, a trip to a holiday paradise, or a gastronomic meal in an exclusive restaurant.

There was a knock at the door. Light raps, as though I'd summoned a ghost with my chattering. Had Martha forgotten something? In any case, I took my time. I went to the bathroom and rinsed my face with cold water.

There was another knock.

It was Dani. She'd brought a bottle of champagne and two glasses with her. She glanced over her shoulder before coming into the room.

"Can't you sleep?" she asked, and kissed me.

"What about Ruth?" I said.

"I'm not here because of Ruth," she said. "Ruth and I are just friends. It's not a big deal."

I looked at her. I didn't believe her. I felt desire. Desire was undeniable. But then I was overpowered by another opposing instinct: at the end of the day, nobody should wish for anything that will hurt someone else.

Dani grabbed my waist. She made to kiss me again, but I twisted my head to the side so her lips—her plump, soft lips—merely brushed my cheek.

"You have to go," I said.

Dani pulled away from me. She hesitated for a few seconds before she realized I was being serious. "I'm not one to beg or plead," she said.

"I know," I said.

"And you do realize that I'll leave the hotel? Is that what you want?"

"You have to go," I said.

TO HAVE DOES
NOT MEAN
THE SAME
AS TO HOLD

I struggled through the deep snow, moving slowly across the slope above the hotel. I had dressed warmly, but still I was cold. The delicate crust shone like magnesium in the moonlight. Tears were streaming down my face. Not for Martha. And not for Dani. But rather, tears of exasperation that I'd given in to a whim, that I had set off on this idiotic and arduous trek, that I was on my way to nowhere.

Even when I was thinking straight, I could let myself be led astray by the most ridiculous ideas. And at any point, I might decide I was in the midst of a crisis, that it was unavoidable, that I was constantly exposed to danger, pain, and oblivion. I felt humiliated, stripped of all honour.

I stumbled and fell. It was as though these fatalistic thoughts had become manifest. I took a wrong step. My foot plunged into an empty space, the loose snow collapsed, and I slid and rolled down the slope against my will. A small, hostile avalanche followed, pushing me from behind. I ended up headfirst in a mass of loose snow and ice and knotted mountain birch too small to be called trees, no more than gnarled tangles, really. It was like a reluctant birth. I fought against it. I couldn't bear it anymore. I didn't want any sympathy. I just wanted to say thank you and good night. I had always thought: this is where it starts. Life. But it never did. There was never enough air between life and me. I couldn't take any more. The Milky Way was burning, burning and blazing white, and I thought I could see strange beings up there, floating, shifting shape—they disappeared and then reappeared. It was as though they were trying to lure me to them. Oh, the temptation. Imagine, to be there in all that vibrating light. Does it not say something about burning seraphim in the Book of Isaiah? That they've got six wings? And is that not so they cover their faces with two, their feet with two, and use the remaining two to keep them aloft?

No matter how tempting it was to die in the snow, under a clear, starry sky, I did not want to leave everything, I did not want to abandon myself. I struggled to free myself, gasped for air, and rolled over onto my back. This simple movement made me proud, and the pride I felt transformed me, made me more alert. It was as though an ancient energy flowed into my body, an energy from both the past and the future. And now that there was so much to think about, there was no space for the original pain. For a moment, I remembered everything, there and then I was able to remember things from the day I was born. Mother screaming. She was happy. Father standing out on the balcony with a cigarette. And Martha lying in a pram, staring at a string of old-fashioned scraps.

The blood pounded in my temples as I rose up from my strange, incomprehensible, little existence. I got to my feet, brushed off the snow and twigs, then remembered something Mother had once said: that she envied the dead, not the living. I don't know if it was a quote from a book or not. Perhaps it was something she'd come up with herself.

I stood there swaying. I imagined small foxes being chased by hares. I was a wandering virgin with oil in my lamp, and my lamp was polished and lit. I spotted two lights down in the valley. They looked like dice made from silver and gold, and they moved and flickered. A strong wind pushed me in the direction of the hotel. It whistled down the mountainside, stacking the snow in drifts and moving the ridges. I thought: fighting your own destiny is a bit like fighting the grammar in a poem.

The wind eased down by the chapel. I was shivering. My clothes were frozen stiff. I stumbled in, sat down on the nearest pew, fumbled with the matches to light one of the candles, but had to give up.

I found myself longing for something to happen, for something to reveal itself in all that glittered in front of me. A small miracle. Was that too much to ask for, when everything else was collapsing? Couldn't the Holy Virgin appear before me? Even if no more than a glimpse. Or what about a donkey? A donkey that nudged me with its muzzle and kept me awake.

I heard Ruth calling, and not long after, the door behind me opened.

"Are you sleepwalking?" she asked, and gripped my arm.

"Sleepwalking?"

"I shouted to you and you didn't answer."

"I was thinking about things," I said.

"Come on," she said, and pulled me up from the pew.

It actually hurt when the heat in the small lobby struck me. It was like melting, like dissolving.

"I hear voices," I said. "Voices talking to me."

"Everyone hears voices here," Ruth said.

"They say that I'm guilty," I said.

Ruth helped me to take off my duffle coat, hung it over the back of a chair.

She stroked my hair, wrapped a blanket around my shivering shoulders. It was a heartfelt caress, and I felt lifted by her touch, lifted by her care that was unconditional, without obligation.

She followed me into the office.

"This is becoming a habit," I said.

"I'll get us something warm to drink," Ruth said.

She disappeared.

I sat down on the edge of the bed, my hands open in my lap, palms up. The church bells rang out down in the valley. It was Sunday. I'd never liked Sundays. Such nonsense that God needed a whole day to rest.

Now I sat there, doing nothing, waiting for Ruth, without the faintest idea of what she would bring, other than refreshments—some comfort perhaps. Her levelheaded, practical presence would be enough, it was all I needed. I heard engines start and cars drive away. Was that a wall clock I heard?

This story started with my sister and me arriving in an alpine village. No, I haven't forgotten that it wasn't an alpine village at all. But when we think back on something that happened in another time, in another era—in our childhood, or few short years ago—then we're forced to make things up. We piece reality together in such a way that it's comprehensible, at least to ourselves. I know that if Martha had told the story of what happened, of this journey of ours, it would be completely different. I'm fully aware of that. Martha's truth may even prove to be the very opposite of mine, and may sound even more sensible in writing.

Once again, I pulled out a book from the pile on Ruth's bedside table, and once again I picked a random passage: "I cannot deny that, on the other hand, this ignorance lent young girls of the time a mysterious charm. Unfledged as they were, they guessed that besides and beyond their own world there was another of which they knew nothing, were not allowed to know anything, and that made them curious, full of longing, effusive, attractively confused."

I wanted to write it down but couldn't face the effort it would take. I felt welcomed in my meeting with these books, this room, this bed with its slightly hard mattress. Welcome. It was like a wound that had got bored and closed up.

And when I now, many years later, remember this time, now, when I'm able to recall the time with Martha, I think first and foremost of a time when our behaviour was driven by vanity and confusion.

NOTES

Monique Wittig, *The Opoponax*, translated by Helen Weaver, Plainfield, VT: Daughters (1976)

Stefan Zweig, *Verwirrung der Gefühle* (1927), in English *Confusion* (Pushkin Press, 2002), is mentioned on pages 72 and 73. Translated into English by Anthea Bell.

Casaubon (on page 16) refers to the priest Edward Casaubon in George Eliot's novel *Middlemarch, A Study of Provincial Life* (1871–72).

The song "Gracias a la vida" (on page 45) was written by the Chilean artist Violeta Parra.

The film about the two blind masseuses, mentioned on page 52, is Hiroshi Shimizu's *Anma to onna* from 1938. The English title is *The Masseurs and a Woman*.

The title "A Door Is Either Open or Closed" on page 57 is taken from Alfred de Musset's play *A Door Must Either Be Open or Closed* (*Il faut qu'une porte soit ouverte ou fermée: comédie en un acte*, 1845).

Death and the Maiden, mentioned on page 72, is Quentin Patrick's crime novel from 1939. The quotation cited here is from pages 307–308 of the edition published by Ljus Förlag in Stockholm in 1945.

The quote on page 91 is from the film *Mr. Blanding Builds His Dreamhouse* (1948).

The quote on page 138 is from Stefan Zweig's book *Die Welt von Gestern* (1944)—*The World of Yesterday: Memoirs of a European*, translated by Anthea Bell (Pushkin Press, 2009).

Photo: Agnete Brun

ABOUT THE AUTHOR

MONA HØVRING is the author of six poetry collections and four novels. Her previous novels include the acclaimed *Something That Helps* (2004), *The Waiting Room in the Atlantic* (2012), winner of the Unified Language Prize, and *Camilla's Long Nights* (2013), nominated for the Nordic Council Literature Prize. *Because Venus Crossed an Alpine Violet on the Day that I Was Born* won the Norwegian Critics' Prize for Literature, was a finalist for the Norwegian Booksellers' Prize, and was included on numerous critics' Best of 2018 book lists.

Photo: Andy Catlin   Photo: Simen Jordsmyr Holm

ABOUT THE TRANSLATORS

KARI DICKSON is a literary translator. She translates from Norwegian, and her work includes literary fiction, crime fiction, children's books, theatre, and nonfiction. In 2019, Book*hug Press published her translation of Rune Christiansen's *Fanny and the Mystery in Grieving Forest*. She is also an occasional tutor in Norwegian language, literature and translation at the University of Edinburgh, and has worked with the British Centre for Literary Translation (BCLT) and the National Centre for Writing. She lives in Edinburgh, Scotland.

RACHEL RANKIN is a poet and translator based in Edinburgh, Scotland. She received a Scottish Book Trust New Writers Award in 2019 and was selected for the National Centre for Writing's Emerging Translator Mentorship Programme in 2018. She has also worked as a tutor in Scandinavian Studies at the University of Edinburgh, where she has taught classes in Norwegian language and Scandinavian literature.

Colophon

Manufactured as the first English edition of
Because Venus Crossed an Alpine Violet on the Day that I Was Born
In the Fall of 2021 by Book*hug Press

Copy edited by Stuart Ross
Type + design by Ingrid Paulson

bookhugpress.ca